AN M-Y E

© (

\

The right of **Vincent Cobb** to be identified as the author of
this work has been asserted by him in accordance with the
Copyright, Designs and Patents Act 1988
All Rights Reserved

A CIP catalogue record for this title is
available from the British Library

ISBN 978-19083722-6-0

Published by
M-Y Books
187 Ware Road
Hertford
Herts SG13 7EQ
www.m-ybooks.co.uk

Front cover and typesetting by David Stockman
www.davidstockman.co.uk

THE PACKAGE TOUR INDUSTRY

2012 EDITION

By
Vincent Cobb

PROLOGUE

This updated narrative of the package tour industry is not intended to provide a historical account of its origins and developments from its conception. That would be a task of monumental proportion and is best left to the academic historians who specialise in researching the details and minutiae associated with such projects. Although I spent the best part of thirty-five years in the package tour field, the period I will deal with in this account covers, generally, but not entirely, what I describe as the dramatic years of 1959 to 1965 or that era between infancy and adolescence. I have also added an important section describing some of the major events that occurred in the industry right up to the end of the seventies.

My story is a personal one, told through the eyes of one of the industry's pioneers, who lived through the early days of holiday travel. I will describe for you the untold hardships of passengers who, many times unknowingly, risked life and limb flying in antiquated, unpressurised, very often World War Two vintage aircraft; when safety was downgraded largely due to ignorance rather than wilful neglect and passengers were generally unaware of their status as the industry's guinea pigs. In the period I refer to it should be remembered there were no 'fan jets' available to the charter sector of civil aviation; in fact, it was only just over a year since the terrible disaster at Munich with the Manchester United football team. The model of plane involved in that tragedy, no doubt for reasons of marketing, had its name changed from the 'Elizabethan' to the 'Ambassador'. Nonetheless, it was the same type of aircraft now carrying package tourists on charter flights.

I will tell you of the incidents I experienced throughout those years, flying in those geriatric planes, and of the interminable delays when a four or five hour wait was considered the norm and it was far from unusual for delays of twenty four hours to occur; and how, during the many hours of frustration passengers had to contend with, they were also faced with the cramped, totally inadequate airport facilities, with limited seating and toilet arrangements. I will also relate the crashes and emergency landings that seemed to be a regular feature of the late fifties/early sixties in the package tour industry, and in which I personally had several hair-raising experiences. I will also describe for you the type of hotels featured in those times, where private facilities consisted of one bathroom at the end of the corridor, where hot water was restricted to a couple of hours a day if you were lucky; air conditioning was an open window and full board catering could mean an invitation for hospital treatment. And when we contracted for hotel accommodation we had to identify whether or not the rooms would be in the main hotel or in the one of many annexes used by even the best of hotels. Because in the early sixties, an annexe in hotel terms meant a room or rooms that could be anywhere up to a mile from the main building and were often in private houses.

I will mention also the experiences on some of the more dubious coach - air holidays, which, in the late fifties and early sixties, were capacious, when it was not uncommon to spend twenty four hours in total discomfort, and then stagger from the coach into a third world hotel on the Costa Brava wondering if your bladder would ever forgive you for your neglect. I will describe the ancient coaches which frequently broke down or suffered punctures in foreign countries; hotel accommodation en route which today even backpacking students would consider insulting, and refreshment stops which, on the frequent occasions on which you were delayed, you would often discover where closed.

Those were the days of adventure, where every trip brought new experiences, usually of an unfortunate nature, where the resilience of our clients, at times in the face of considerable distress, encouraged the phenomenal growth of package tours. The industry has much to thank the travelling public for, as it was essentially their indefatigable thirst for travel, their insatiable appetite to visit new and exotic places, that was responsible for laying the foundation of what was to become an immense multi billion pound enterprise, employing hundreds of thousands of people and ultimately enriching the lives of millions. I hope you find the narrative interesting, and if I may have given the impression that holidays in the early days were fraught with misery and discontent, then I truly apologise. The stories I have told are factual and did actually happen, although in some instances I have deliberately changed participants' names to avoid embarrassing them. Allow me also to apologise if some of my dates might be questionable - memory is not always reliable but, nonetheless, that does not make the events I describe any the less true! The truth is that the pioneers of this industry were themselves undergoing a learning curve and very largely were circumscribed by the facilities available to the market, such as obsolete aircraft, inadequate hotels that had simply not been designed for holiday makers and, probably worst of all, the almost total lack of communication throughout Europe which prevented the companies from quickly resolving problems. And if our clients did experience suffering and hardship it certainly was not borne out of indifference. It is a fact that we appreciated the continual support of the travelling public; in the main they enjoyed the experiences and the novelties and if the contrary had been the case then the package tour industry would have suffered a very early demise, instead of becoming the sophisticated giant it is today.

On a closing note in this narrative there may be people of today's generation who will doubt the authenticity of these incidents; let me inform them that what I have described actually did happen and any doubts will in no way dilute the factuality of these events.

The Package Tour Industry

CHAPTER ONE

1959 THE EARLY DAYS

I began my 'career' in the travel industry during the summer of 1959 with a small Blackpool travel agency with the now perhaps misleading name of Gaytours! I managed to persuade the owner, a Mr. Norman Corkhill, to take me on in a position, which he felt, was only suitable for a female; I mention that only to illustrate the extent of my enthusiasm for joining the travel industry as it was then. At the time I was twenty-four years of age, married with a young daughter, and had a semi detached house with a mortgage we couldn't afford. My initial wage at Gaytours was the princely sum of ten pounds a week. To try and overcome our financial difficulties we let the 'front' room and one of the bedrooms of our house to a young couple like ourselves. Even so, life was hard. I spent most of that first summer either dealing with theatre tickets for Blackpool holidaymakers or travelling between Blackpool and Southend on one of the coaches we organised for our coach/air holidays to Jersey.

In addition to processing theatre tickets we also had responsibility for handling incoming passengers from a National firm, called Lunn's Tours. Every Saturday I had to stand at the local bus station and wait for the arrival of coaches say, from Huddersfield, or distances in those days we would describe beyond the horizon. Then I had to carry their suitcases – no one could afford taxis – to their boarding house, which, hopefully, was not too far away. A particular Saturday that is permanently etched in my memory was when I met two couples, who had never met before, and had to take them to the boarding house quite nearby. Exhausted, after carrying two lots of suitcases, we arrived at the boarding house; I knew the owner having met her on previous occasions. She welcomed the visitors and asked me if I would carry the cases up to their room. (Notice I said room) The room we arrived at had two double beds and the landlady said, 'This is your bedroom.'

'What?' The cry was heard. I think it was one of the women. 'You mean we have to share the same room?'

'Of course,' the landlady replied. 'Why? Is something wrong?'

'But we've only just met. I mean, we don't know each other.'

There was a simple smile from the landlady as she said, 'No, but you soon will.'

As I left she said to me, 'I had to do that 'cos I was overbooked.'

Later, the couple telephoned Sir Henry Lunn to complain and they were transferred to a smart 3 Star Hotel on the promenade.

During that summer, aside from the theatre tickets and seeing the shows, free, I spent most of the time meeting clients at the bus station, transferring them to their hotels, (I should say Boarding Houses) and then seeing them off on various coaches, mainly Standerwicks, to the Lake Districts, Southport, and even to the Isle-of-Man. It was a great summer. I remember that famous, infamous, landlady, a few years later, when she travelled on one of our end-of-season tours from Blackpool, the local airport, to Mallorca. She insisted on the very best of rooms at our hotel, with Cordon-bleu meals and as my old boss said at the time: "She has a rolls appetite with a tram car budget."

He was absolutely right.

In those days we also organized Coach-Air Holidays from Blackpool all the way to South end Airport and from there on DC3's to Jersey; it was a round trip of over five hundred miles - the return journey taking place overnight. Sometimes, if I was lucky and the ancient DC3 aircraft from Channel Airways, we used wasn't full, I was privileged to fly to Jersey, immediately turn round, and fly back again to Southend. On the Sundays when the flight in either direction was full, I had to sit it out in Southend Airport for about three or four hours until the returning passengers landed and we set off on the return coach journey through the night. It was hard work, excessively hard work, particularly as I had to be in the office again on the Monday morning, almost immediately after arriving in Blackpool. But I thoroughly enjoyed it. I enjoyed the freedom, the variety and above all the sense of adventure I felt each time I undertook a journey. By the end of that summer I had more or less become a permanent fixture around the office, and in Jersey with our Reps and the airport staff, and, increasingly, Norman trusted me with greater responsibility. So much so that when our end of season holidays for the Blackpool Landladies took off in the October, I was given the job as courier to escort a party down to Southampton to join up with the Bergen Line cruise ship to Madeira. It was to be my first experience in 'diplomacy'. It was in the October of 1959 and the ship was known, notoriously as, The 'Vomiting' Venus.'

It was a lovely morning that Friday in October very unusual for Blackpool. At that time of the year it was normally much wetter and windier than we were used to in the summer months. It was a very exciting day for me. As I mentioned, I had been charged with taking a party of Blackpool landladies (they insisted on being referred to as 'hoteliers!') to connect with the Bergen Line cruise ship, the Venus, from Southampton. We were scheduled to fly from Squires Gate Airport on a twin engine Viking aircraft to Gatwick, where we would meet up with a second, smaller party of hoteliers from Jersey and then coach the group down to Southampton Docks. The package tour industry in those days was virtually non-existent. In point of fact the name had yet to be coined; it was generally known as 'the travel industry', which covered every aspect of travel including the railways.

Airports were largely unchanged from the Second World War which, effectively, meant passenger facilities consisted of a collection of old Nissen type huts and sheds. The aircraft in which passengers had to fly in at that time were of the same vintage; I remember flying in one particular DC3 which still proudly displayed bullet holes down one side of the fuselage. They were, for the most part, twin-engine propeller planes, with dodgy old seats, unpressurised and violently uncomfortable in bad weather, which was fairly frequent given their height limitations – their ceiling was restricted to 7 thousand feet. They also had a limited flying range, which in turn required one, sometimes two, re-fuelling stops on the Mediterranean journeys. But all this was of no concern to me. I now, rather arrogantly, and presumptuously I might add, regarded myself as part of management and I was living a great adventure.

Quite unbelievably we took off on time from Blackpool that morning. Everyone was in a good mood, which meant no one had yet complained. After an uneventful flight, which I found quite disappointing, I was looking forward to some stormy weather, we landed at Gatwick Airport at approximately eleven o'clock, and hit our first problem: the Jersey flight was delayed by fog but hopefully it should clear within the hour. So we had to wait, something Blackpool landladies are not noted for. It was ten minutes before the first one started moaning - lucky I had been warned.

"Ere! What's going on? What the bloody hell's happening?' It was one of the older women, a particularly nasty piece of work in her late fifties who wore a permanently angry scowl on her face.

'Well, as I explained on the flight from Blackpool,' I began, 'we're meeting up with a flight from Jersey and then we'll all go in the coach to Southampton. It shouldn't be too long.'

'You've no bloody right to keep us here waitin' - you've got to give us refreshments! And just how long are we going to wait, anyway?'

I had no instructions about paying for refreshments, so I overlooked her insistence. 'Look,' I said, 'why don't you go for a cup of tea and put your feet up, we should only be about an hour.'

'You're payin',' she demanded.

'I'm afraid not. This is what is known as a 'force majeure", you know, an Act of God. So we can't be held responsible.'

She went off grumbling and I learned my first lesson about complaining Blackpool landladies; never give in to their moans or they'll literally have you for breakfast! And so that is how the rest of the trip continued. The Jersey flight eventually landed a little after twelve, no big deal in my book, but Christ, you should have heard the Blackpool contingent complain. Finally I shepherded the passengers onto the coach - the Jersey clients were exceptionally nice people, something I was completely unprepared for, and we set off for Southampton, about an hour away by road. It was just after one o'clock as we entered the suburbs of the town; it was then that a deputation of the Blackpool group approached me. The same woman from the airport was amongst them, a Mrs Hodgson, I later learned.

'You know what time it is, don't you?' I checked my stainless steel Timex watch, "One o'clock.'

'Yeah. And it's dinnertime. When do we get us dinner?'

I was a bit stumped at that, I had to admit. So I said, 'You'll get lunch, (I was becoming quite sophisticated by then, dinner was something you had in the evening!) on the ship.'

'We will hell! By' time we get on' ship and shoved our baggage away, they'll have finished serving. So we'll miss out on a bloody meal. And that ain't a force whatnot, it's your fault. So what you gonna do about it?'

I checked the Bergen Line documents again: embarkation at 1400 hours, ship sails at 1500 hours. We still had plenty of time, and having been on the phone to the office from Gatwick, I was authorized, if it came to it, to provide them with a 'cheap' lunch. So I directed the driver to find the cheapest restaurant he could, which turned out to be a pub, and I arranged a simple set meal for them all. Soon there was a brief respite from the complaining, as the driver and I found a quiet corner in the pub for a sandwich. Then came the monumental task to get them all back on the bus; they were well into the booze by then. It was a quarter to two before I managed it, and just after two when we turned into wharf thirty-two, from where the Venus was sailing. It was then I noticed one small further problem: the ship was pulling away from the dock without us on it. Panic stricken I grabbed hold of an old local 'salt' to ask him where the Venus was going. I thought it might just be changing berths.

'The fackin' ship's sailin',' he grinned.

'Well get the fackin' thing back,' I shouted in horror. I had thirty-two passengers on the coach who had paid a small fortune for their holiday, and who now had nowhere else to go. I turned to look at the group fully expecting uproar, and was pleasantly surprised to see them all sitting there in open-mouthed silence. They were literally gob smacked! Rather fortuitously, I had experienced something similar a few years earlier when I spent some time in the Merchant Navy as a Boy Rating. Two of us, overindulging one night in one of the many pubs on Commercial Road, which bordered the length of the King George the Fifth Docks where our ship was berthed, we were late getting back. When we did eventually return to board the ship we discovered, to our intense amusement, that it had already sailed and was on its way down the Thames. A friendly dock policeman pointed us towards the offices of the Port Line handling agents, who very reluctantly gave us a lift in a tender; it wasn't really fortuitous because the tender had to go down the Thames to pick-up the Pilot. We managed to board the ship in the Thames Estuary, at the same time as the pilot was disembarking, and escaped with a warning from the First Officer.

So I contacted the handling agents of the Bergen Line in Southampton and explained the problem. Eventually they managed to make radio contact with the ship, and the Captain agreed to halt the ship, which by then would be about three miles down the Solent. A rather smallish tender, I would say it was no longer than twenty feet, appeared, and, with a lot of pushing and shoving, we managed to crowd everyone on board. The landladies meanwhile uttered not a single word. Among the Jersey passengers were two disabled teenage girls and, given that the weather had taken a turn for the worst and that we were now hitting quite a strong swell, I was concerned as to how we would be able to transfer the two girls from the tender onto the rolling deck of the Venus. To make matters worse it was dark by the time we finally caught up with the cruise liner and even with all the lights at maximum visibility it was quite difficult. The gangplank had been lowered and the boson was stationed at the bottom. We had to wait until the swell of the river moved the tender close to the gangplank, and then physically 'throw' the passengers across the gap. It was extremely dangerous - not helped by the jeering passengers lining the upper deck of the Venus. In one instance the boson missed a Blackpool woman and she half fell into the river. What a bloody performance! In all it took the best part of an hour to transfer everyone except the two disabled girls. The only answer we could come up with to solve that problem was to tie a rope around each of their waists, and from there to the rail of the tender, while its pilot and I each took an arm. We then had to suspend them over the side until the two boats were virtually touching, at the same time praying that the boson would catch them. The girls, to their credit, thought the whole affair was hilarious, the opposite of their guardian, who stood halfway up the gangplank shrieking that we were trying to kill them!

Transferring the luggage took no time at all but I was somewhat bemused to see a couple of cases, the only casualty of the adventure, floating off down the Solent. It was nine o'clock at night before the operation was completed and I now had to face the added problem of how to get back to Blackpool. The original plan was for me to return on the same coach to Gatwick and then catch the scheduled flight I had travelled on that morning, back to Blackpool. Now that was all up the spout! But all that was mostly irrelevant compared to my relief that we had avoided a disaster. My final memory of the experience as the tender headed back to the dock was of Mrs. Hodgson, perched on the top deck of the Venus, shaking a fist at me and screaming, 'You haven't heard the last of this, Cobb.'

I never knew whether or not she heard me, but I shouted back at her - from the safety of the tender 'Well, you're the greedy cow who wanted 'us' dinner!' I was quietly delighted to learn some time later that one of the missing suitcases, floating off down the Solent, did in fact belong to Mrs. Hodgson! We never did solve the confusion of the mix up in sailing times. Bergen Line insisted it was our fault for not translating British Summer Time to GMT, and tried to bill us for an extra meal for all the passengers and crew. We told them, not at all politely, I might add, to sod off, and challenged them to show us on the passenger tickets where it mentioned Greenwich Mean Time. The matter was dropped, but not forgotten, as Mrs. Hodgson had let me know in her farewell speech.

By the time we docked at Southampton again it was half past ten at night; needless to say the coach had long gone, and I still had to find a way home before morning. I was due to fly to Majorca at nine o'clock the next day on a charter flight from Blackpool. I had no idea how I was going to make it. Then one of the customs officers offered me a lift to the station with the suggestion that there still might be a train to London. Thankfully he was right. I caught it with five minutes to spare but I now had no means of letting anyone know where I was or what was happening; we didn't have a telephone at home in those early days and there was no such thing either as direct dialling, so I could hardly have phoned the boss from the deck of a tender! I got to London at about half past midnight, indulged in the luxury of a taxi to Euston, and managed to make the night train to Glasgow, which stopped at Preston. I caught the milk train from Preston, arriving in Blackpool at about six in the morning; I phoned Norman Corkhill from the station and told him what had happened, thinking he might go through the roof. I remember his words to this day: 'You're in the travel business now, Vincent. You just have to cope with these little problems!'

'Bastard', I thought afterwards. He might at least have shown a little bit of sympathy. But as the years passed and my experiences of the industry grew, I came to realise he was correct in what he had said. I walked home from the station, just as Pat, my wife, was feeding our twelve-month old daughter. I barely had time for a cup of tea, a piece of toast, and a shave before Norman arrived to take me to Squires Gate Airport to catch the charter flight to Palma. I hadn't been to bed, and had managed only a couple of hours' sleep on the train, but the excitement and adrenaline of actually flying to Spain kept me going. Besides, I could hardly allow my unsympathetic boss to know I was bloody exhausted, could I?

CHAPTER TWO

THE FIRST CHARTER FLIGHT TO SPAIN

It was the same aircraft that I had flown into Gatwick on the morning of the previous day: a thirty-four seater, twin engine, unpressurised and extremely uncomfortable, Vickers Viking. It had a crew of three; Captain, First Officer, and a stewardess, who soon informed me I was expected to help. The weather in Blackpool that morning was back to its normal self; black skies, heavy rain and gale force winds. Norman soon had a heated discussion with the pilot because he was refusing to take off in what he described as 'atrocious conditions'. We genuinely couldn't understand what the hell he was going on about; why should a bit of Blackpool weather prevent us from flying? I learned that day: you simply did not argue with Norman Corkhill he was far too devious and manipulative ever to lose an argument. Finally, at around three o'clock that afternoon, without the weather abating, the Captain was persuaded, in the interest of his job, that it might be advisable to concede and agree to take off. Such a thing today, of course, would be inconceivable, but in 1959, the Civil Aviation Authority didn't exist: a body known as the Air Transport Advisory Committee or the ATAC for short governed the aviation industry. The role of that August body was not related to the safety aspects of aircraft or flying in general; it was more a governmental protective body set up to ensure that competition for BEA and BOAC, the nationalised carriers, remained non-existent. So it wasn't that difficult for Norman in the end to convince the Captain of our Viking aircraft to take off in the Blackpool storm, as the Captain described it, helped by the inevitable deputation of complaining Blackpool landladies. My thoughts at the time, I remember, were thank Christ I didn't have to deal with them again! So, the boss and the complainers combined, you could say, were largely instrumental in us taking off that afternoon in a forty mile an hour gale. Needless to say, it was rough from the second we were airborne, something we almost didn't achieve as I watched the port wing avoid scraping the ground by inches. And rather like the incident the previous day with the old 'Vomiting Venus', the passengers were frozen in silence, as the stewardess and I sat there grinning. We were facing a flight time, if we included the stop we would need for re-fuelling, of about seven hours, in what the Captain informed us from his forecast, was likely to be one of the worst storms that year. And because we had no pressurization we would be flying right through the centre of it!

'You'd better let the passengers know,' he advised me. 'Tell them to remain seated with their safety belts fastened tightly. And Tracy,' he added, turning to the stewardess, 'you had better forget the coffee and sandwiches for that lot...' pointing in the direction of the passengers, 'Just make sure you have plenty of sick bags.'

'What about you and Nick?' she asked, nodding towards the co-pilot.

'Leave it for about an hour or so. We'll be crossing the northern coast of France then and it will be dark, so you'll be able to turn off the lights.'

'Where are we re-fuelling?' I asked.

'I was originally routing for Toulouse but with the force of this headwind I've had to change it to Lyon. It's going to be a rough ride.'

'Is it likely to be as bad as this in the Bay of Biscay?' He looked at me curiously.

'It's always rough in that area. But it's nowhere near our routing. Why do you ask?' 'No reason really. It's just that I know some people on a cruise ship who'll be going that way shortly.' I had Mrs Hodgson very much in mind.

'Well, that's one place I would not like to be,' the Captain muttered. Serve you right, you cow, I thought, as images of her throwing up while whinging, passed through my evil mind. Tracy and I went through the cabin towards the crew seats at the rear of the plane, glancing at the pale faces of the passengers on the way. No one spoke although one of the elderly women grasped Tracy by the arm and thrust a used sick bag towards her. I got the hell out of the way, it was dangerous territory. Forced to hang on to the edge of the seats as we made our way to the back, it was like riding a bucking bronco. Then the plane chose that precise moment to drop like a stone for a couple of hundred feet, which sent Tracy flying dumping the contents of the sick bag over one very unfortunate man. It certainly didn't help matters when I started to laugh, especially as it coincided with a couple of the passengers screaming as we were hit by a bolt of lightning. It looked scarier than it actually was, but if you had enjoyed a misspent youth as I had, on Blackpool's famous Pleasure Beach, to say nothing of winters in the Merchant Navy storming through the North Sea, you would be well used to this kind of thing. I was still chuckling when I reached the back of the plane and almost fell into one of the rear facing crew seats. Tracy had gone back to try and clean up what she could - I for one didn't envy her. When she finally joined me, the cabin lights dimmed, and the only sound we could hear was the filling of more sick bags. 'I suppose the crew will want their coffee now,' she complained. 'We're crossing into France. Would you like one, Vincent?'

'Yeah, thanks. That would be nice.'

'You wouldn't like to give me a hand, would you?'

'Sure,' I said, following her into the tiny galley. It consisted of a small sink bordered by stainless steel cupboards on both sides and a space between of no more than two feet in width. 'Have you heard of the "Mile High Club",' she asked innocently as she plugged in the coffee pot. I shook my head.

'No, I haven't. But then I've only been in the travel industry for a few months. What is it, this club?' She grinned wickedly. 'Well, to become a member you have to have had sex at least one mile above the earth.'

'Great! How about yourself. Are you a member?'

'No. Not yet.' She pushed herself against me suggestively. 'But I've always wanted to join.'

So there I was, a happily married man, in the centre of a violent storm, high above the ground, being propositioned by a stewardess who must have been out of her mind to even consider sex at a time like this. And this was 1959, for God's sake, an era where all the nice girls were virgins. Fortunately, we were interrupted by a scream from the cabin. One of the old dears had a nosebleed.

'Don't panic,' Tracy said to her sternly. 'It's a nose bleed not a heart attack.' She glared at me is if it was my fault and then ordered me to bring the first aid kit from the galley. I dutifully obliged and we spent the next hour or so mopping up a mixture of blood and vomit in between trying to cope with the aircrew's incessant demands for bloody coffee. 'Look, Tracy, you see to the passengers, I'll try to make the coffee.'

'I'm running out of tissue and sick bags,' she complained.

'Then we'll just have to let them get on with it, won't we?' God knows how long it took me to make it, as my wife Pat would tell you, at home I could hardly boil water but I was buggered if I was going to spend any further time watching that lot engaging in a symphony of vomit. I just managed to make it to the flight deck with the coffee when Tim, our undaunted skipper, informed me in his matter of fact voice that we were about to begin our descent into Lyon. The rain was lashing down and, if anything, the wind was gusting at a higher rate of knots than when we took off from Blackpool.

'Jesus,' I managed to say as I watched the both of them fighting with the plane for control. 'Yes. You'd better take a seat.' He gestured to the spare seat in the cabin, and I thought what a privilege to be allowed to sit where I could actually witness the landing. 'Don't worry,' Nick, the co-pilot tried to assure me. 'We'll try and get it down in one piece!' The old wartime spirit I guessed. What they didn't realise was that I had little sense of fear in those days I genuinely believed I was blessed with an innate sense of stupidity, something that was to serve me in good stead in the years ahead. 'Oh gosh!' I remember saying sarcastically, 'aren't we lucky to have you flying the plane.'

'Piss off!'

'Knock it off you two. Nick, keep your mind on the job.' He began to read off the altitude; it seemed to me that the lower we descended the worse the weather became, and for the first time I wondered if I had left my wife any insurance.

'Flaps twenty five degrees,' Nick said, followed shortly by, 'Undercarriage down, flaps at fifty degrees.' I heard a voice through the radio detailing the runway heading and the wind speed I was sure he said gusting at thirty knots, but I didn't think it was the right comment. We came in like a crab, drifting from one side to the other, constantly hit by the crosswind and almost blinded by the rain lashing against the windscreen. We almost missed the runway and it was only due to a last minute correction by the Captain that we hit the deck safely, about three hundred yards further down the concrete than we should have done. 'There,' I said to Nick, 'That wasn't so bad, was it?' For the first time he gave me a grin. 'Next time you can have a go!' We taxied towards a cluster of huts, which, I was informed was the Lyon Passenger Terminal not much different from Blackpool really. We all squeezed into the one bus, and managed to get soaked going from the bus into the terminal. I was in the process of ordering a coffee in fractured French when the Tannoy announced that the airport was now closed! We were well and truly stranded. There was no transport to take us into town, and even if there was, no one had any money, at least between the crew and myself, to pay for accommodation. I chatted briefly to the Captain about the prospects of the weather lifting. He seemed quite relieved that the airport had closed and informed me with profound insight that we would just have to make the best of it until the next day. In the meantime, he and my friend Nick were taking a crew minibus into Lyon centre to arrange a hotel; evidently, without the required rest period they would be out of hours in the morning and we could be stuck here longer still. Tracy was going with them, leaving me with the responsibility for the beaten but not bowed passengers. Another bloody great night without a bed! I went round apologising to everyone and suggesting they do what I was going to do settle into one of the uncomfortable seats, or on the floor if they preferred it, and try to get some sleep. To add to their discomfort, the guy behind the bar suddenly pulled down the shutters and declared it also closed. That's when they began complaining again, about how much they had paid for this holiday, and how they wouldn't dream of treating guests in their 'hotels' with such indifference. No coffee, no food, nowhere to sleep. On and on and on, until finally I had had enough. 'Listen you lot,' I shouted. 'I'm as sorry about this as you all are, but you can't blame Gaytours for the bloody weather! You can see for yourselves that everything is closed, so you'll just have to do the same as me, stop your moaning and get on with it. Now, you can either try and make yourselves as comfortable as possible,' I gestured around the empty passenger lounge with its sparse seating, 'or you can all spend the night complaining to each other about how badly you've been treated. Only don't bother me; I haven't been to bed for two nights now and I'm damned if I'm going to have you lot pestering me. Is that clear?'

It worked! Although I distinctly heard a couple of them threaten me with the ultimate sanction of solicitors. The best I could manage was lying on the floor using my jacket as a pillow and dozing between cigarettes. And then, at five in the morning when the airport cleaning staff arrived, I had to queue behind the women who had commandeered not only their own toilet but also the men's. So it was a knackered, dirty and unshaven me who climbed aboard the craft for the final leg to Palma. Not a single one of the passengers was speaking to me, making it quite obvious that I was to blame for their discomfort. Of course I regarded it as a hell of an adventure; bloody hell, they'd just spent the night in France, hadn't they? They should have been charged extra! The sector from Lyon to Palma, skirting the edge of the Pyrenees and from there over the city of Barcelona, was uneventful. The weather had changed for the better and when we landed, some three hours later, the passengers seemed to be in a better mood which judging from the night before was not very difficult. I spent an hour on the ground with our Head Rep, a rather arrogant Spaniard called Manuel, listening to all his complaints about the hotels and, more vociferously, the low breed of clients we expected him to deal with these days (I was quickly coming round to the view that all everyone wanted to do was complain.). I remember asking him if he was related to royalty, he was acting so bloody superior! The landladies might have been a moaning bunch of minnies, but basically they were just ordinary people who had worked hard all summer in their 'hotels' and they deserved a holiday. The last thing they needed, I told him, was a supercilious courier who treated them with contempt. I then invited him to resign, which shut him up immediately; that was after he informed me he would be reporting me to Norman Corkhill.

'Join the fucking queue,' I suggested. A couple of hours later we were airborne again, on the way back, so I believed, to Blackpool. We had been in the air about an hour when my good friend Nick emerged from the flight deck and woke me up to tell me we were going to Gatwick. Evidently Norman Corkhill and the airline, Pegasus Aviation, had decided between them, earlier that morning, that because of the overnight in Lyon, it would mean that the aircraft would have to spend what was left of the Sunday laid-up in Blackpool, whereas a divert to Gatwick would allow the airline to fit in an additional charter. So, Norman got a reduction in the price and I got dumped in Gatwick with instructions, yet again, to make my own way home. This time I was lucky, I made it home by train, by midnight on the Sunday. At least I would be able to spend the night in a bed! I did learn later, accidentally as it happened, that Norman had no intention of paying for the Gatwick/Blackpool sector, with me as the only passenger. A pity though, that he hadn't warned me.

CHAPTER THREE

1959 -1960 OVER THE TOP

I 'repped' on a further three flights during October and November of '59, all of them on the Viking. The first was an uneventful trip, again to Palma, with the plane actually taking off on time. After flying in a cloudless sky, and a fuel stop again at Toulouse, we landed at San Juan Airport on schedule. One or two of the landladies did manage to complain because we hadn't provided them with a hot meal. I informed them politely that this was more like a delicatessen than a café. The only slight hiccup was when I asked our Head Courier, Manuel, to sign a receipt before I would hand over the two thousand pounds Norman Corkhill had asked me to give him to pay for outstanding hotel bills. He tried to refuse, alleging that I didn't trust him and that, in effect, I was insulting him. When I told him he was correct, that I didn't in fact trust him, he went bananas. This time it was his turn to threaten resignation, but after a lot of huffing and puffing, he finally did sign it. I couldn't have cared less because I had already arranged for Nuria Gaze, a courier who had just joined us, to settle the bills. He snatched the cash from me and stormed away. I didn't think any more of it but, a few days later, after I had given the receipt to

Norman and in turn he had telegraphed Manuel to ask him why the bills hadn't been paid, we received a telex from Manuel denying that I had given him any money. Bastard! It was fortunate I had had the sense to insist on a receipt. Norman finally managed to contact him by phone after the inevitable four-hour wait and casually informed Manuel that if the bills were not settled immediately he would bring in the Guardia Civil. That was a bit like threatening a Russian with the KGB. Needless to say, the hotels were paid the same day. Norman promptly sacked Manuel and promoted Nuria Gaze to Head Rep

The second flight I was on was a two re-fuelling stops trip to Malaga. At least that was the schedule, as that type of aircraft, due to its lack of pressurization, was unable to fly over the Pyrenees. The first touchdown was to be Lyon, the second at Perpignan. Unfortunately, after a five-hour delay, it looked as if we wouldn't make Malaga that day because Perpignan was due to close at eight o'clock that evening. We prepared the passengers for the possible night stop, with the promise, that overnight accommodation would be arranged for them (at least Norman did, I don't think he trusted my diplomatic skills). Even from my limited experience, I didn't believe this promise for a second. Technically, the airline was obliged to pay since the delay was their responsibility. However, in those impoverished times it was a battle to persuade the airlines to pay even for light refreshments. I was correct. As the passengers were boarding the plane, Norman took me slyly to one side and informed me that I had the time between Blackpool and Lyon to come up with a plausible excuse why the hotel accommodation would not be available. 'Christ, Norman. What am I supposed to tell them?' I gasped, only partly in disbelief.

'Oh, you'll think of something,' he assured me confidently. 'It'll be a test for you anyway. See if you've got the backbone for a career in this business.' Then he pointed a finger at me in warning. 'But you don't let them know it has anything to do with Gaytours. Understand?' I nodded as the stewardess closed the door behind me. I was already beginning to sweat when the plane took off. What on Earth was I going to tell them? How about the hotels were all full? Or the Airline hadn't been able to get through to them? Hardly plausible. I needn't have worried though. An hour or so into the flight, the Captain asked me to go up front for a word. He was a short man who seemed to have difficulty fitting into his seat, while his head barely reached the edge of the windscreen. I was tempted to suggest it might be better if he sat on a cushion, but for once I bit my tongue.

'Mr. Cobb – Vincent, isn't it?'

'That's right.' 'Well, you do know we have a problem with Perpignan, don't you?'

'I know it closes at eight-o'clock. Why?'

'Are you asking me why it closes at eight? Or what do I want?' He laughed at his own joke. I sighed. He may have shot down God knows how many German bombers, but he would hardly be a candidate for the Intelligence Corps.

'What is it you want, Captain?'

'The First Officer and I have been discussing the situation and we have a proposal to make to you.'

'Really? I'm all ears.'

'Okay. You may or may not know it but this type of aircraft does not have a pressurization system and because of that we cannot technically fly over the Pyrenees. Were you aware of that, Vincent?'

I nodded. 'What's your point, Captain?'

'The point is, my dear fellow, that if we were to fly over the mountains, we could then change our first tech stop from Lyon to Toulouse and from there fly direct to Malaga. There would then be no need to have a night stop. Are you with me?'

'I hear what you're saying but I'm not altogether sure I understand. Surely, either we can fly over the bloody mountains or we can't? Which is it?' He looked uncomfortable for a moment. It didn't last long. 'We, that is, the First Officer and I, are suggesting that we ignore the pressurization problem, we climb to sixteen thousand feet, and we cross the Pyrenees at the lowest point.'

'I'm sorry,' I admitted, 'I don't understand the technicalities. What happens if we do that? I mean, is it safe for the aircraft?'

'Oh, yes,' he assured me. 'It's perfectly safe for the aircraft. It might cause the First Officer and myself a bit of a problem with breathing, but...' he reached over to where two cylinders were clasped to the side of the cockpit, 'we should be okay if we use these.'

'Great. But what are the passengers going to use?'

'Well, that's the problem really. It's not a big deal, though. I mean, it's not as if they'll be flying the plane.'

'So, how will it affect them?'

'Well, we suggest you don't say anything to them, then we won't have any hysteria. One or two of the older ones may experience some disorientation, nothing to write home about - but if you haven't told them they'll think it's a normal part of flying. What do you think, Vincent?' How the hell was I supposed to know? A little bit of discomfort seemed to be well worth it for the time it would save. And it would certainly solve the problem of the hotel accommodation.

'Well I'm willing if you are Captain. But it has to be your decision.'

'Good. I'll re file the flight plan to Toulouse. I'll talk to you later.' It turned out to be one of those never to be forgotten experiences that you should never ever consider repeating. For a start, the average age of these landladies was about fifty-five which to me was pretty old and which meant that quite a few of them were well over sixty. After re-fuelling at Toulouse, which fortunately no one questioned, I was on the flight deck watching the mountains materializing out of the moonlight, when I got the first call from the stewardess. One of the elderly passengers was suffering from an ear bleed and she wanted to know if it might be serious. The Captain assured her it wasn't; I think he had less medical knowledge than I did. He just didn't want the inconvenience. By now we were employing the oxygen cylinders, taking it in turns for a whiff. It was too late to turn back now. 'Put some cotton wool in her ears,' I suggested to the stewardess. She left, shaking her head, only to return almost immediately. Two more passengers were suffering from heavy nosebleeds and another appeared to be having some kind of a heart attack. The Captain handed her one of the cylinders. 'Here,' he said, irritably. 'Share this between them. It's only for another thirty minutes or so, then we can begin descending.'

'What if she dies?' she asked with genuine concern.

'Well, we'll just have to bloody well hope she doesn't, won't we?' he snapped. I then considered that he was the one becoming disorientated, his head kept rolling from side to side and he appeared to have lost control of his tongue.

Fortunately, the First Officer also noticed it. 'I've got the Con. Skipper.' When there was no acknowledgement, he reached across and gave the Captain a hard shove on the shoulder. 'I said I've got the Con. Captain.'

'Yeah right,' he mumbled, 'you've got the Con.' And thankfully he took his hands away from the column. 'What about that passenger?' the stewardess insisted.

'Come on,' I said, climbing out of my seat. 'Let's try her with some oxygen.' The woman was half in and half out of her seat when we got there, with her friend stroking her forehead and making soothing noises. Her eyes were closed and she was obviously having difficulties breathing. So was I when I thought about it, I hardly had sufficient breath for a smoke. 'We'll have to put her on the floor,' I said. I remembered reading that recently in a Frank Slaughter novel, although what you did after that I had no idea. That wasn't in the book. We were in the process of laying her down when a voice from behind her said, 'Can I help? I used to be a nurse.' I turned around to discover a rather nice looking woman, probably in her early forties, and with blood pouring from her nose, bending down to assist us. 'Fluff a pillow under her head, and then loosen her blouse.' The stewardess was happy to oblige. The passenger then knelt down and administered the oxygen. 'You do know what is causing this, don't you?' she said. 'No, I'm not a medical man,' I said with feigned innocence 'Is she going to be all right?'

'Not unless we lose some altitude quickly, no, she definitely won't be all right. Why are we flying at this height anyway?'

'Do you know about 'planes?'

'Yes. I was in the RAF during the war. And I do know you're not supposed to be flying at this altitude without oxygen, especially if you're her age. So why are we? And aren't those the Pyrenees down there?'

'Yes,' I admitted. 'I think the Captain is trying to save some time.'

'I don't understand. I thought we were meant to be spending the night in Perpignan? Don't tell me he's taking a short cut over the mountains?'

'Well, I believe he's flying over the lower peaks. That way we can make it direct to Malaga.' She leaned forward and whispered in my ear. 'Well you go and tell him if he doesn't lose us some altitude quickly this old lady here will probably die. And if that should happen then I will do everything in my power to ensure he faces criminal charges. Do you understand?'

Not another one? I thought. Asking me if I understand as if I was some kind of moron. I left her without responding and made my way up front again. 'We have a passenger who is in danger of dying unless you can get this plane to lose some altitude,' I snapped at the First Officer. 'Good timing,' he commented dryly. 'I'm already bringing her down to twelve thousand feet. That should help. How bad is she is?' I told him about the ex-nurse who was looking after her, and how she was threatening to bring criminal charges against the Captain. The co-pilot waved a hand towards him. 'It's no good talking to him. He's out of it.' He was right the Captain seem to have disappeared into a world of his own; he kept trying to grab the oxygen cylinder from his First Officer. He was breathing almost as badly as the lady in the cabin. 'Serves the bugger right. He shouldn't have misled me, he never told me this kind of problem would happen.' He shrugged philosophically.

'He also lied to you. He told you we'd be flying at sixteen thousand feet in fact, for the last half an hour we've been at nineteen thousand.' 'Look, why don't you go back and reassure your nurse while I start the descent. The quicker we lose height the better for all of us.' I did as I was told, but the ex-nurse still wasn't too happy, accusing the Captain of irresponsibility; something, I had to admit, that had crossed my mind. She also enlightened me by stating that the ceiling for the Viking was supposed to be only seven thousand feet, and that twelve thousand could still cause breathing difficulties. Obviously, the last thing I was going to mention was the real altitude at which we'd been flying. At that moment the aircraft went into a descent mode, and some minutes later the old lady lying on the deck started to come to life again as her breathing improved, although she continued to show signs of distress throughout the rest of the flight. The remainder of the journey passed without further incident and, two and a half hours later, we landed safely at Malaga Airport where an ambulance was waiting to take both the old lady and the captain to the hospital where they were to spend two nights before recovering from their ordeal. I couldn't have cared less about the Captain but I was relieved to learn that the passenger recovered a few days later. We heard that from the hospital but we never heard from her again; she must have thought it was quite normal for her to be fainting.

As the passengers were disembarking, still in ignorance of the drama, the ex-nurse made a point of sticking her head into the flight cabin. 'You do realise you only just got away with it, don't you?' she said, accusatorily, to the Captain. I think it was all he could do just to nod his agreement. His face was as white as a sheet and he looked badly shaken. The First Officer turned from his seat and shook me by the hand. 'Thanks for your help,' he said, genuinely. 'I don't think we'll be doing that again.'

So I got to spend the night in Torremolinos, the beach resort where the clients, (now they were off the aircraft they had ceased to be called passengers!) were spending their holiday. I remember staying with the aircrew at a hotel called the Pez Espada, the Spanish for swordfish. For the first time in my life I was wining and dining in four star hotel luxury, something I thought only existed in James Bond novels. I got to sleep in a huge bed, in a double room to myself. And in the morning I actually had a view of the sea. I couldn't believe it!

Needless to say, the return flight was delayed while we awaited the arrival of a substitute pilot. When we eventually took off, later that afternoon, the flight went strictly according to plan, stopping for fuel at Perpignan and then Lyon. The passengers all seemed to have had a good holiday so, remarkably, there were no complaints about the extensive delays. I thought then that sometimes we got things right! We had a bit of a bumpy ride after we crossed over Paris and a couple of the passengers were sick but that was almost immaterial. We landed at Squires Gate Airport, more or less to the revised schedule, and surprisingly in dry weather. The only disappointment for me was that the boss wasn't there to meet us; I half hoped he would have made a point of acknowledging my enterprise during the trip. But obviously he had more important things to do. I learned later that he was flying around the airport in his own private plane!

CHAPTER FOUR

THE WINTER OF MY DISCONTENT

Since, in 1959/60, the holiday section of the travel industry was very much in its infancy, it meant in effect I had to become a 'jack of all trades'. In the October and November period, as I mentioned, I was looking after the Blackpool landladies on the flights but from then on and throughout the winter months I had to carry out a whole variety of different jobs each of which in today's package tour industry is highly specialized. I began by learning about the design and printing of holiday brochures. This included the photographic side, making sure we had the most flattering even if misleading photos of the hotels we were featuring next summer. Sometimes, when Norman fancied using a hotel, because it was well known in our limited market or it looked quite exotic, we would include it in the brochure, despite the fact we had been unable to negotiate a contract. In other words, we had no beds. Did I mention that at that time there was no such thing as the Trade Descriptions Act? I also got to go across to Ostend a number of times in the winter months to tie up hotel accommodation for our programme of coach/air holidays. The hoteliers there were always pleased to see you and couldn't be more helpful, which made the task so much easier. The exciting part of going to Ostend was the ferry rides each way in and out of Dunkirk. It was like trying to keep your balance on an unpredictably moving floor. I remember once treating myself to a cabin on the overnight return crossing and I was literally thrown out of the bunk. That hadn't happened to me since my Merchant Navy days, and it brought back some interesting memories. Norman, however, took himself off to Mallorca that winter to negotiate for hotel allocations through a local Spanish agency. We had arranged a series of flights for the summer by Viking aircraft again (God help us!) by circumventing the licensing regulations, which I described earlier. The way round the problem was to involve different travel agents, including ourselves, in applying for a series of three consecutive charters, the permitted maximum before the anti-competition rules were triggered. This way we were able to mount what was known as a 'back to back' series, solely on charter flights, and consisting of a weekly flight to Palma from Manchester for twenty one or twenty two weeks throughout the summer. To make a living those days in this industry it was necessary to be as devious as Norman was! Finally the 1960 summer brochure was finished sometime in the late January. It was only a twenty-four page, two-colour brochure, there were very few four colour jobs printed at that time, and it then became my job to arrange distribution to the travel agents. There was no point, either, in organising a mass circulation because quite a number of the agents were refusing to sell our holidays; snobbery amongst the agents was rife at that time and in the eyes of many of them we were just a pretentious little company with no pedigree. Most of the Agents at that time were in IATA, which was a licence to sell air tickets.

So all the brochure deliveries had to be carried out by road, which in the winter, when you have to cross the Yorkshire Moors, sometimes in a blizzard, wasn't exactly a barrel of laughs. I remember once getting stuck in a snowstorm on Snake Pass, a very dangerous link road between Manchester and Sheffield. On one side there was a steep drop of two or three hundred feet down into a valley; a slight skid and you were dead. Miss the road on the other side and you would hit limestone cliffs. It was my own fault. The police had been giving out warnings all day to avoid the area but I hadn't done very well with the East Lancashire agents that day and I was anxious to try my luck with the Yorkshire ones. Visibility was virtually non-existent, so I was crawling along, shivering with the cold (the heater on the 'shooting brake' we had hired wasn't working) when I hit a snowdrift. All I could see by the car lights was a mountain of snow in front of me and when I tried to reverse I sank deeper and deeper into it. It was about five o'clock in the evening, pitch dark, freezing cold, and I was obviously going nowhere. I tried to make the best of it by convincing myself I had intended to spend the night in the car anyway. I had brought my shaving kit and a towel so I would be able to use the public toilet facilities, wherever I could find any, so all it meant was instead of the car being in Sheffield it was on the Scenic Route. But as the Heater wasn't working, there was little point in leaving the engine running. I turned it off and climbed amongst the holiday brochures in the back. And there I was, surrounded by 'sunshine' and freezing to death! The best I was able to do was doze off occasionally; looking back, I'm sure that had I really fallen asleep I would have died from hypothermia. At around four o'clock the following morning I saw headlights through the rear of the car and I thought I would get out for a look to see if I was being rescued. I couldn't even open the door. It was jammed against the snow that must have accumulated during the night. I heard voices telling me to stay where I was - a bit of bloody daft advice, I thought at the time; where the hell did they think I was going? It was an hour or so later that I realised they were not as daft as I had assumed. The driver of the snowplough had attached a chain to the rear fender of the shooting brake and reversed me out of the drift, while his partner had come forward to shovel away the snow from the front. It was only when I was able to climb out that I realised it was only the snow blocking the front wheels that had stopped me from plunging down the cliff.

Then of course, it was their turn. They played absolute hell with me, telling me I was a damned maniac, and didn't I know the road had been closed since mid-afternoon the previous day? I played the innocent. I didn't have a radio and I had no way of knowing, and besides, I was a stranger to the area. How was I to know how dangerous it was?

'But anyway, fellows, I'm really grateful for your help. And if you're clearing the road, is it all right if I follow you the rest of the way to Sheffield?' I won't tell you what they said. They managed to turn me around and then pointed me back in the direction of Manchester with a final kind of piss- off gesture! I was off like a shot, very relieved, I might add. That was just one of many similar incidents that winter- as the boss was constantly reminding me: The joys of the travel industry. Once, driving into Halifax on frozen roads and almost bald tyres, I lost control of the shooting brake and slid sideways down one of the many steep hills leading into the town, ending up inside a bus shelter! But I did manage to sign up more than one hundred travel agents by the middle of February; these were in addition to the agents already selling our holidays. So the next couple of months was spent in the office taking reservations on the phone, setting up an administration system to deal with the bookings, doing the accounts - something I had had training at - and travelling yet more, each evening, around the Lancashire towns for presentations to audiences arranged by local agents. It was a long hard winter, with many nights on the road. At the end of it, and remembering my experiences with the Blackpool landladies, I was coming to the conclusion that this travel industry was more suitable for insomniacs and mentally disturbed people, rather than the normal run-of-the-mill inhabitants. But it had not been a very successful booking season. The best seller turned out, not surprisingly, to be Jersey; we weren't too worried about the Ostend programme because clients shared the same coaches as the Jersey holidays and we could place them on the Channel Airways scheduled service from Southend. It was the Palma series that was the most worrying hardly what we would call a success. I played around with the numbers and came to the conclusion that if we were to cancel one of the series and turn the programme into a fortnightly rotation, then we might just avoid a disaster. Cancelling everything would surely have meant bankruptcy for Gaytours and I would be out of a job. So we took a risk - or at least Norman did - and went with it. I wrote to all the clients on alternate weeks offering them a similar holiday on either the previous week or a week later than that which they had booked. I don't believe we had a single cancellation; in fact, I gained the impression that foreign holidays were so novel that a change in departure date only added to the excitement! So we were able to begin the Palma programme by late April of 1960 by kicking off with, would you believe, a preseason flight for the Blackpool landladies. I was growing quite fond of them by then.

CHAPTER FIVE

Summer 1960 'HOUSE OF ILL REPUTE'

What a dump Manchester Airport was but what an exciting dump! I believe if you had asked anyone that particular year what an airport passenger terminal was they wouldn't have known what you were talking about. That was simply because they didn't exist. I think I mentioned earlier about the worn, wooden Nissan huts; well, allow me to amplify. There was no heating, which didn't matter very much in July and August but it did for the rest of the season. There was no such thing as a coffee shop or a gift shop or any kind of shop. If I remember correctly, there was a kind of stall where you could buy newspapers and cups of tea and stale sandwiches, but very little else. There was a restaurant of sorts but that was only for the rich BEA passengers, certainly not for the 'peasants' on charters. There was very little seating, other than the floor, with which I was personally very familiar. Again, it didn't matter too much whether the aircraft operated on time, but as we soon discovered, that was to become something of a miracle rather than the norm. So the airport 'lounge' very quickly became a cattle pen and it was that, in my view, which contributed more than anything to the outbreak of client complaints. It became so bad that by August people were literally sitting outside on the tarmac. And of course everybody smoked in those days, myself included, so if you were stuck inside the airport 'huts' it was almost impossible to breathe. I flew out on the first charter to Palma to check on all the arrangements with the hotels and excursions and to give the couriers a bit of on the ground training. It wasn't unlike the blind leading the blind! I didn't really have much of a clue about reps, and excursions, but one thing I was fast learning from Norman Corkhill was bullshit. As he frequently used to say, 'Try to convince them you know what you're talking about and you're halfway home. Because there's one thing for sure - they sure as hell won't know!'

As the first charter of the season it was to be something of a 'maiden flight' for Gaytours. This was the first time we had operated out of Manchester, so we were particularly anxious that everything should go well. Well, if you regard a scheduled take off of nine am finally departing at two o'clock as going to plan, then you would be correct. The only favourable aspect was that with a refuelling stop scheduled for Toulouse, there would be no question of that airport being closed on arrival. So finally we landed at Palma Airport at eight in the evening and the coach was still there waiting for the clients to transfer them to their hotels. As I have already pointed out, for that particular summer my boss, Norman Corkhill, had contracted all of the hotel accommodation. It should be borne in mind that the Majorca of 1960 was completely different from the one of today. At that time, there was very little 'beach type' accommodation for instance; Palma Nova and Magaluf were largely deserted beaches, whilst Arenal had only two hotels. It was still the accepted tradition that when the father of a family died, the best land went to the eldest son. So he inherited the farm and the remaining sons, if any, were given the valueless beach land bordering Palma Nova, Magaluf and Arenal, as a kind of sop. Today the eldest son is broke, whilst his brothers are all millionaires! But those resorts were for the future. For now clients generally stayed either in areas such as Terreno and Calamayor, or, which was in the majority of cases, in hotels in the old part of the town, in what was effectively the commercial quarter, certainly not suitable for tourists?

I got a call at about ten o'clock that night from Nuria Gaze, now our Head Rep, asking me if I could meet her at the Hotel Peru, a rather dubious establishment located in one of the squares, or plazas, in the heart of the Old Town. I hadn't had the opportunity of inspecting any of the town hotels that Norman had contracted; I merely assumed that he knew what he was doing far better than I did when it came to hotels. I couldn't have been more wrong! The Peru was a dilapidated building with half of its front balcony hanging in mid air, rather like a distressed passenger hanging on for dear life to the ship's rail on the Titanic. It had a front porch, which was covered in dirt and debris, the front door wouldn't close fully, and two of its downstairs windows were badly cracked. And all this was before I had stepped inside the building!

'Is it as bad as this inside?' I asked Nuria. She looked at me in some embarrassment, and then nodded. 'I did tell Mr Corkhill, when he was here last week, that I thought this was not the place to put our clients.'

'What did he say to that?'

'He told me I was too fussy, and for the price we were paying it was good value, and that the clients would appreciate the Old Spanish character of the hotel. But I haven't told you the worst yet.'

'I take it the clients didn't agree with him, about the character I mean?' She shook her head. 'It's not just that, Vincent. The problem is they're not even in the main hotel.' She pointed towards an alleyway across from the main building. 'They're in there, eight of them, four couples, and I have to tell you it's totally uninhabitable. I think you had better see for yourself.'

I followed her into the shabbiest of buildings, up three flights of unlit staircase, and met the clients on one of the landings outside what appeared to be a bedroom of sorts. I noticed one lady was in tears. When I glanced inside the bedroom I could understand why. For a start it was gloomy, and the only natural light was a window that looked out onto a wall; it appeared not to have been cleaned for months, and when another lady silently pulled back the covers on the bed for me to have a look, I almost threw up. It was quite literally crawling with bedbugs. One of the husbands then invited me to check the bathroom, just off the landing. The bath was discoloured by a black coating. I couldn't make out whether it was caused by age, or simply dirt. The toilet was completely blocked and out of commission. Even the most desperate case of gastro enteritis would have been hard pressed to have used it. 'Jesus!' was all I could think of to say - at the same time wondering just what the bloody hell Norman was thinking of. The main hotel was grim enough but this annexe was positively offensive. I vowed there and then I would never ever let Norman Corkhill anywhere near hotel contracting after that. I was even more annoyed when I discovered that Norman hadn't actually visited the hotel when Nuria first complained about it. Evidently he had contracted hotels on the suggestion of a local agent whose only brief from the boss was, 'the lowest possible price.' All I could do was to apologise. I was completely unable to offer any explanation but I do remember saying that under no circumstances could they remain there.

The problem then was where on Earth were we going to put them? Until Nuria informed me there was a small hotel, recently opened, and situated by the tennis club in Son Armadans, that she had been in touch with and which could accommodate all of our clients. So we helped them downstairs with their luggage and organised taxis for the transfers. Nuria and I went with them. By now it was quite late, so it had to be the New Hotel or sleep on the beach. Fortunately it was an excellent alternative. Nuria had phoned ahead and the proprietor was waiting for us. The hotel had only fifteen rooms on four floors, but would you believe it had a lift! There was a small but attractive dining area, with a lounge/bar leading off it. It was also in a pleasant location, particularly after the Peru, and the owner spoke very good English, which also helped our weary and somewhat pissed-off group.

A bit later, we were having a coffee in the bar, and I endeavoured to negotiate a reasonable rate with Miguel, the owner, (why was I surprised when we had to settle at three times the price of the Peru?) when we recounted the story of the Peru to him. He began laughing at just the mention of the name. He then proceeded to inform us that the Peru was a mix between an old commercial hotel and a notorious Old Town Brothel, mostly inhabited by middle-aged prostitutes, whose only clients were lonely and somewhat desperate commercial travellers. Miguel went on to say that anyone who was from Majorca would have known that. He had no knowledge of the annexe, but as he said, there was no way he would put a foot inside the hotel – he had his reputation to think of! Dear old Norman had surpassed himself. He had actually – sight unseen, but with the help of a local so-called travel agent – contracted a dilapidated brothel for the whole of the summer season. I still found it hard to believe that he had failed to visit the place. No one in his or her right mind could actually step inside the dump and then proceed to sign a contract!

That night the owner had arranged a celebration for the opening of his new hotel. I went with Ramon Adell, who was the manager of a local agency and who became one of my closest friends. When he asked me how I was and I told him I was 'knackered', I asked him what was the Spanish for that phrase?

'Estoy Jodido,' he replied.

So I practised and practised. It was pronounced: Estoy Hodido.

Thinking it meant 'I'm tired' I repeated it to the owner at the cocktail party that night; he was there with his wife and a number of friends. There was a shocked silence and the owner took me to one side. 'Did you realise what you have just said?' he asked me.

'Of course, I said I am tired.'

'No. what you just said was: I am fucked.'

Jesus, I could have killed that Ramon. I apologised to the party and explained it was a misunderstanding. They actually laughed.

The following day Nuria and I inspected the remaining hotels we had on contract for the summer season. A second hotel was also situated in the old part of town, and while it was at least clean and quite pleasant, it was a commercial hotel totally unsuitable for holidaymakers. Another was located in an extremely narrow street, opposite the cathedral, which was impossible for coaches to negotiate, which meant that clients would have to carry their own luggage. It was also a lodging house for the island's various entertainers, who by now were flocking in as news of the developing tourist market spread. This in time meant that that the pension's bar stayed open most of the night and when the entertainers returned in the early hours of the morning, it was used as a rehearsal room, much to the annoyance of our clients who were trying to sleep. Yet another hotel was situated by the sea on the road to Ca'n Pastilla. It had a nice outlook but as well as being in the middle of nowhere it was bang next door to the Gitanos (gypsy) encampment and clients were constantly disturbed by the noise and the pervasive smell of cooking, to say nothing of widespread break ins. Almost daily the police had to attend the hotel to deal with disappearing wallets and/or passports, which were a valuable commodity in those times.

What all this meant to me, even with my limited experience, was that we did not have a single suitable hotel in which to accommodate the poor unfortunates. I was also afraid that by leaving them in the remaining establishments throughout the summer we would be pressing the self-destruct button. I couldn't help but wonder just what Norman had been doing during the two or three weeks he had spent on the island; he most certainly hadn't been visiting hotels. So, with the help of Nuria, we began scouring the areas near Palma, close to the sectors where the hotels for the Blackpool landladies were located, obviously not as up market, but at least away from the commercial centres. In other words as far out as Ca'n Pastilia itself, then along the Paseo Maritimo, which was the equivalent of the Promenade, and over towards the small beach resort of Calamayor. It took us the best part of a week but in the end we managed to change every one of our remaining hotels. Of the replacement hotels, we continued to feature two in our Majorca programme for over ten years after that summer. They were both three star hotels: one was the Costa Azul, situated on the Paseo and within walking distance of the city, the other was the Hotel Calamayor an extremely nice hotel where I became close friends with the manager, Pablo

Ripoll. We arranged for appropriate photographs to be taken and I did the written descriptions. It was my intention, when I got back to the UK, to carry out a modest re-print and redistribute the brochures, together with an explanation about the changes, to our travel agents.

Norman managed to contact me on about the third day to ask me what I thought I was playing at? He in turn had received a telex from our Spanish agent complaining that I had cancelled all the hotel accommodation. So I asked him if the agent had told him why I had cancelled the hotels.

'He hasn't got a clue,' he said grumpily.

'Why don't you ask him what he was doing recommending that we contract rooms in a brothel?' I said. There was a measured silence; I really believe he was as shocked as I was. 'Where did you get that news from?'

'Norman, it's common knowledge over here. And I've been to see the place and I wouldn't put a rat in there. It's absolutely disgusting. Have you seen it? Or did you contract it sight unseen?'

'Well, I didn't actually see it, no, but it was a bloody good price and the agent recommended it. Are you sure it's a brothel? They're not kidding you over there, are they?' I remember sighing, it was all you could with Norman.

'Take my word for it. No one is kidding us; in fact we're something of a laughing stock in Palma. So I cancelled the contract. Then I went to have a look at the other hotels. Norman, we're tour operators not commercial travellers. There isn't one of those hotels that are suitable for holidaymakers. I don't know what the hell that agent was thinking of. Anyway, I've found suitable alternatives they're a bit more expensive, but I can tell you all the clients are grateful. And they've stopped complaining. So...' I went on before he could stop me, 'I've arranged photos of the new hotels, and I'll bring them back with me so we can send them on to the travel agents.

'I also thought, while I was here, that I could have a look at contracting for next year if that's okay?' He spluttered then as if he was stuck for something to say. 'You're taking a lot on yourself, aren't you? We haven't even decided next year's programme yet, how do we know how many beds we need?'

'Well, I take it we'll be featuring Majorca again, won't we? And if I assume we'll be contracting at least the original number of beds we had for this summer and if I top that up a bit, I don't think we'll have any problems. Do you, Norman?' I think he had one eye on the cost of the call because he suddenly said, 'Well you seem to know what you're doing, so I suggest you get on with it. But don't pay too much!' I breathed a sigh of relief. I had his endorsement and it had proved pretty painless.

And so I became a hotel negotiator, obviously with a great deal of help from Nuria. In fact another lesson I had learned was that in what was to become the constant search for additional hotel accommodation, in an increasingly competitive market, the best intelligence we could employ was that of the couriers. They were the ones with their eyes and ears to the ground; they were the ones that immediately spotted any available opportunity. And I used them unsparingly from then on.

After that, I spent most of the summer of 1960 travelling across Spain, principally to Mallorca and Ibiza and on to the Costa Brava, negotiating with various hoteliers and travel agents, and signing contracts for the following year. The first thing I did was to change the Mallorcan travel agency Norman had recruited - the one responsible for the previous hotel contracts. I made contact with a couple of agents and eventually decided that we would work with a company called Viajes Taber, who had branches in most parts of Spain, and whose head office was in Barcelona. Since my telephone conversation with Norman Corkhill about hotel contracting, my geographical brief had widened considerably. The change of hotels we instituted for the current season proved very successful, and load factors on the aircraft improved to the point where it now seemed as if we would finish the year in profit. So, as a result, coupled with what we now knew was going to be an expanding market for 1961 with some new competitors appearing on the scene, we decided to extend our programme to include Ibiza, the second largest of the Balearic Islands, Mainland Spain was also included, which was one of the reasons why I had chosen Viajes Taber, and also a small programme of holidays in parts of Italy.

At the time I felt it was far too ambitious; rather like making a quantum leap. One thing I quickly realised was that it was bloody well killing me! Every three weeks out of four I was on the move, travelling by now all over Europe, by plane, by train and coach, and by car, even occasionally by boat. Rather like my earlier trips with the Blackpool landladies, it was not uncommon to have to go one, sometimes two consecutive nights without sleep.

I remember arriving in San Sebastian one particular night, in the middle of a tremendous thunderstorm, to find that the resort was full with Spanish tourists; not one single hotel vacancy, until I encountered a very nice lady who owned one of the smaller establishments and who invited me, if I was desperate enough, to sleep in the downstairs bathroom. It was damned uncomfortable but I was very grateful, especially when she refused to charge me. At that time we were working with an Agency called Viajes Iberia; they represented us in San Sebastion and I became close friends with the owner, Miguel Fluxa. He was quite a character, a handsome looking man who attracted all of the attractive looking females. Miguel actually lived in Mallorca

– there is a story to tell about him and his then partner that I will come on to later. In the meantime I contracted various hotels along the San Sebastion coast ready for our coach/air holidays the following summer. Needless to say the sale of the holidays was a disaster and we had to cancel the whole programme.

From there I flew to Barcelona to meet up with Claudio Hoyos, the son of the owner of Viajes Taber. He was to accompany me on the contracting trip along the whole of the Costa Brava. I hadn't met him before, but he appeared to be a pleasant enough young man of about the same age as myself, and he spoke fluent English, which was a relief. From Barcelona we headed by car to a resort called Calella de la Costa, a bit of a drab place with a number of old hotels and some new ones under construction. It was a beach resort but the snag was that the railway line cut across the road and the beach, making it quite dangerous. But the hotels were not bad and they were incredibly cheap, so we signed two or three contracts. After finishing up there we travelled on to Blanes and then Lloret de Mar a resort which had been growing rapidly for some time as a result of the coach tours coming in from the UK. In fact I gained the impression that every tour operator under the sun was in Lloret scrambling for hotel accommodation (it wasn't exactly a shock therefore to discover the following year, that nearly every UK Company was featuring the same Lloret Hotels! In fact, as events transpired, it became evident that the resort was more than three hundred per cent oversold.). After Lloret de Mar, it was Tossa de Mar, then Estartit; the whole contracting period lasting for almost fourteen days, quite a lot of the negotiating with hoteliers having to take place late into the evening because of their work schedules. I was picking up some tiny bits of Spanish on the way; Claudio gave me lots of lessons.

CHAPTER SIX

BENIDORM

Finally, a totally exhausted Vincent met up with Claudio's father, who was known rather affectionately as 'El Zoro Viejo', or the Old Fox, at a resort called Palamos at the far end of the Costa Brava. Here Claudio took his leave of me with the arrangement that he would meet me later that night at Barcelona railway station where I was scheduled to catch the night train to Valencia and then on to a newish resort called Benidorm. Apparently the old man was interested in purchasing a hotel in Palamos, called the Mozart, and for some reason wanted my input on its suitability for the holiday market. I thought it was a nice hotel, back from the beach, but in its day, quite modern, and I informed Sr. Hoyos of my opinion. He seemed pleased and, communicating mostly in sign language - no one spoke a word of English and I still only spoke little Spanish - I found myself joining a group of fifteen people around an outside table at a local restaurant. It was the most frustrating dinner party I think I had ever endured. The meal might have been okay had I known what I was eating; the same might have been said about the company at the table had I known what they were saying. I spent an almost speechless evening, not understanding a word and not being able to say a word. I felt a monumental bloody fool. Once or twice, some of the guests attempted to talk to me in French, but all I could do was to shake my head. I used to believe my French was fractured; that night I discovered it wasn't merely a hairline fracture it was positively compound!

I couldn't wait to get away, thinking that that would at least give me a breather. I couldn't have been more wrong. As we were leaving the table and various people were saying goodnight, I felt myself being ushered by the 'Old Man' towards his car. Unfortunately, it wasn't the car I had arrived in which was about to be driven away by one of Taber's drivers. It also contained my suitcase. I did my best to communicate with Snr. Hoyos and with sign language explain that my luggage was on its way to God knows where, but he simply didn't understand as I watched it sailing off into the moonlight. Jesus, I thought. Now what? There was no question of going all the way down to Benidorm (wherever that was!) without any luggage, but there was not a thing I could do about it until we arrived at Barcelona railway station and I could speak with Claudio. I cursed him for leaving me in a situation where I was totally helpless and when we arrived at the station that was the first thing I told him. There was a further problem. It was by now the early hours of Sunday morning and the offices of Viajes

Taber would not re-open until the Monday morning. That in itself might have been irrelevant were we able simply to go to the driver's home to collect the suitcase but unfortunately no one was sure where he lived! Claudio thought he might be able to find his farmhouse, and since I was lost without luggage, we set off in search of it. Eventually, three to four hours later, after riding around in the hills outside Barcelona, we found him and then nearly broke down his front door to wake him up. Suffice to say I recovered the case, returned to Barcelona station, and caught the eight am train to Valencia. Another sleepless night and, to add to my miseries, the train was incredibly uncomfortable, noisy, slow, and completely lacking in dining arrangements. I did manage to buy a couple of sandwiches when we stopped at one of the numerous stations en route but was buggered if I knew what was in them since, again, the labels were in Spanish! Something I needed to get used to.

It was ten o'clock at night when we finally arrived in Valencia after fourteen hours on that damned uncomfortable train. Next, I had the job of persuading a taxi driver to take me to Benidorm, a journey of a further three and a half to four hours – there was no airport close to Benidorm other than Valencia. I only managed it in the end by paying him money in advance. Like the UK there were no motorways in Spain at that time, so it was three in the morning when we arrived in Benidorm and, would you believe, I couldn't find a hotel open! The only bit of French that hadn't deserted me, yet again came to mind: 'Deja vu!' I made another silent vow to myself that night, trying to stretch out on a concrete bench facing the beach: Come hell or high water I was determined to learn this bloody language and never again would anyone be able to put me in these kinds of situations.

It began to get light at around five am so I decided to have a tour of the town. Actually, in 1960 there wasn't that much of it. It was still a small fishing village, with the main street climbing up to the inevitable Spanish church perched on a promontory above the sea. On each side of the promontory were the most magnificent beaches I had come across so far throughout Spain. Even in the morning light the sand sparkled beside the waters of the Mediterranean and was the colour of gold. I don't think I had ever seen anything so beautiful since stopping for a couple of days in Tahiti when I was in the Merchant Navy. It occurred to me then that this was a resort with enormous potential - rather an understatement given the uncontrolled developments in later years. But at that time it was a very pretty village, oozing with old world Spanish character and catering for only a limited amount of tourism, since the nearest airport, Valencia, was some four hours away by coach. A local bar/coffee house opened at around six that morning, and as well as providing some much needed food, the owner, who did speak a little English, was kind enough to let me use the bathroom of his upstairs apartment. So at least I was able to make myself a bit more respectable when, at nine, I went along to the office of Viajes Taber and met the manager, an incorrigible rogue called Manolo Torrubia. What a jack the lad he was! He came closer to a cockney 'spiv' than anyone I had ever met, or would be likely to meet, in London! He was also very likeable and given that he had the energy of an express train, he whizzed me around Benidorm identifying the small number of existing hotels and (mostly) pensions, and showing me round the substantial building work that was taking place. Manolo also informed me that there were plans to extend Alicante Airport, which at present was just a grass field airstrip. That in itself would trigger off a massive development programme. And of course he was right. It was his timing that was wrong because it was years before Alicante Airport was refurbished sufficiently to take the larger aircraft. I left Benidorm two days later, having stayed in the Avenida Hotel on the main high street, and caught up with my sleep. It wasn't only hotels I inspected during my stay; I was also shown the ambitious plans for two nightclubs, new restaurants and coffee bars and a new innovation in those days - a country barbeque. I met the mayor, a man positively enthusing about the future tourist prospects for the resort. Many years have passed since I last visited Benidorm and I doubt I will ever see it again. Even in the late sixties and the early seventies it had become quite an enormous city with high- rise apartment blocks, hotels almost touching each other side by side along the beaches, and bars and discos on every corner. I often wonder what that mayor who I met all those years ago might think of Benidorm today and whether this was what he really wanted to happen.

Personally, I still miss the lovely old fishing village.

CHAPTER SEVEN

LATE 1960 TO SUMMER 1961
OVERSEAS AVIATION

The summer of 1961 saw a favourable development: the relaxing of licence applications due to the advent of the ATLB. The Air Transport Licensing Board, change over from the old ATAC. Of course there was still a strong element of 'protectiveness' towards BEA but the new establishment was much more liberal in the granting of licences. As a result we were able to introduce considerable expansion into our '61 Summer Programme which in turn enabled us to contract for the Argonaut, a seventy four seater DC4, made in Canada under licence during World War Two. The aircraft was fitted with Rolls Royce Merlin engines, had a longer range than its smaller counterpart, and was supposedly pressurised. Once again it took a trip over the top of the Pyrenean Mountains to convince us that the damned pressurisation system was worse than useless. As was the company owning and operating the planes. It was a new company called Overseas Aviation, Jersey based, presumably for tax reasons, although its operating base was Gatwick Airport. On some of the less popular routes we continued to feature the Viking aircraft, and also Derby Aviation's DC3, where we had transferred the coach/air tours to Jersey from South end Airport to Derby Airport.

On a personal front, I kept my promise to myself and enrolled for a Spanish course that winter at the local technical college. When the numbers in the night class fell to the level where the tutor informed us he would have to cancel, I 'recruited' volunteers from the office to join me in my studies.

The summer of 1961 was remembered mostly for the endless chronicle of prolonged delays affecting almost every flight where the Argonaut was involved. In terms of time-keeping the season was a nightmare from start to finish. Pretty well every single day we were hit with a delay of some sort. The weekends were the worst, when we suffered the inevitable accumulation of delays sometimes stretching to over twenty-four hours. The Argonaut was old and obsolete; maintenance procedures were highly questionable and spare parts for the plane hard to come by. It was no surprise either to the aircrew or to the engineers servicing the planes that breakdowns were such a common occurrence; it was their considered opinion that all of the aircraft should have been grounded for a complete overhaul. Mac, the chief ground engineer at Ringway, suggested their rightful place was the knackers yard. On the whole our clients were philosophical, taking the problems in their stride. But eventually even the resilient British spirit had had enough, especially when there were a number of delayed flights in addition to ours, causing intolerable suffering as passengers were crowded like cattle in the airport terminal. I believe the factor that added most to the misery was an almost total lack of information from the airline. It seemed that no one from Overseas Aviation was on operations duty at the weekend. They did have a representative at Manchester Airport, a very likeable and very frustrated guy named George Fleming, who, like ourselves, was unable to gather any information about any particular aircraft, where it was or what the problem was. Sometimes the aircraft would actually be sitting on the ground, at Ringway, broken down, probably waiting for a part to arrive from Gatwick. If we were lucky or very quick, we might catch the aircrew before they beat a hasty retreat from the airport, to demand information from them. Invariably all we got was a shrug as if to say: 'Gatwick are supposed to be sending a part in the next few hours, so what the hell do you expect us to do?' But whenever we tried to phone Gatwick there was never any response.

One particular flight I remember well, scheduled to fly to Barcelona, was some sixteen hours late. On this occasion the aircraft was parked at Ringway and a new crew had been summoned from their Stockport hotel something we had bullied George Fleming into doing. They were a bit pissed off because, as they told us, they were not due to fly until later that night and then it was supposed to be a Venice flight. Finally a deputation of passengers led by the inevitable barrack room lawyer approached us. It was a guy in his late thirties, balding, wearing glasses and looking absolutely furious.

'What the fuck's going on?' he demanded aggressively.

'That's charming,' I thought. 'We've been at this airport now for over fifteen hours and we still have no information.' I let Norman deal with him apart, from being the boss, he was more diplomatic than I was.

'Have you come across to ask me for some flight information or just to abuse me?' Norman said politely.

'Well, we demand to know what's going on. No one is telling us anything and you lot don't seem to care.' I didn't think it appropriate to inform him that I had been at the airport now for the last twenty hours.

'If you would like to come with me,' Norman said, 'I can show you where your aircraft is; it won't help though because it's broken down and the engineers are still waiting for a part to arrive from Gatwick. Are you coming?' he asked, walking away. 'We're not interested in looking at a broken down plane,' he almost snarled. 'All we want to know is when will it be ready to take off?' Norman looked at him thoughtfully. 'Yes, of course you do.

And I can understand that. Look, I've had an idea. I'm going to speak with the crew again, see if we can't arrange something. Leave it with me will you. I'll be back presently.' This seemed to satisfy the group leader. At least it helped to confirm his authority. 'Come on, Vincent, let's see what we can do.' As we passed into the staff only section I asked Norman what he was hoping to achieve by speaking to the crew? 'We're not going to speak with them,' he replied. 'So where are we going then?' 'We're going to the staff canteen for a cup of tea and a bit of peace.' He waved a hand at me impatiently. 'You're beginning to sound like that lot in there Just leave it with me. I know what I'm doing.' That quickly shut off any further questions I might have had, so we spent twenty minutes or so with our tea and toast before returning to the overcrowded passenger lounge. They were still waiting for us, a look of almost eager expectation on their faces.

'Well?' the leader demanded.

'Yes. Well, I've a word with the pilot as promised and I've explained the situation to him; I've also told him how angry you all are. And do you know, he sympathises and he's asked me to put a proposition to you.'

'What kind of a proposition?' the client asked suspiciously

'The pilot says to tell you all he fully understands why you are upset, and furthermore, he's prepared to do something about it.'

'Like what?'

'Well, he says that if you are prepared to take the risk so is he. And if you're agreeable we can take off in half an hour.' There was a stunned silence at this. I had to turn away so they wouldn't see me grinning.

'What does he mean exactly by taking a risk?'

'Just that really. He's still missing the part from Gatwick, and he'll probably have to fly on three engines, but he says that shouldn't be too much of a problem. And anyway, if it is, he reckons he should be able to make it to Gatwick Airport, with a bit of luck. So, what do you think? Shall I tell him to call the flight?'

'Is he mad?' The leader spluttered. 'He wants us to take off on three engines?' 'Actually, no, he doesn't. But like he says, he's as fed up as you all are, and he hasn't been to bed for two nights, so the quicker he can get the flight under way the better.' I thought that was laying it in a bit thick, two nights without sleep and he wanted to fly the plane!

'Well you can tell him to fuck off,' he snarled. 'He's not taking risks with our lives. We'll just have to wait for the part to arrive, won't we?' He nodded towards the rest of the group, who glared at us in stony silence.

'As you wish,' Norman said. 'But don't blame me, will you. I've done the best I can for you.' And with that they all walked away, grumbling still, only now they had a new target.

'That was priceless,' I told Norman. 'I shall remember that for when I write my memoirs.'

'It's all about psychology, Vincent. Something you'll have to learn in this business.' The aircraft finally took off about three hours later and not a word from our clients. It still didn't prevent me from feeling sorry for them though; eighteen hours they had waited for this flight in the most cramped conditions imaginable. And to make matters worse, I think Norman was tempting providence when he made reference to the aircraft getting as far as Gatwick Airport if anything were to go wrong, because that is precisely what happened. Half an hour out from Manchester one of the engines did pack up and the pilot was forced to divert to Gatwick. The poor buggers were there for another eight hours.

The Package Tour Industry

CHAPTER EIGHT

THE LONG WEEKEND

The season went on with no let up in the constant delays that by now had become an almost daily part of our lives in the industry. Day after day, weekend after weekend, I virtually lived at Manchester Airport, my constant companion being exhaustion as a result of the endless nights without sleep. But I couldn't give up, I wouldn't give up; apart from having nowhere else to go and expecting our second child in the August, I had no money and we were only just managing to keep up the payments on the mortgage. And in any event, I kept telling myself, it wasn't as bad as the war years when hunger was a major factor. And at least I didn't have to wear clogs!

One particular weekend, towards the end of July, the bubble finally burst, and the continued neglect by Overseas Aviation caused a crisis of major proportions. As was usual, the weekend began for me on the Friday evening, when after finishing at the office, I set off for Manchester Airport to catch the Argonaut flight to Palma, hopefully on time to keep some important appointments with hoteliers. The flight was scheduled for take off at 1900 hours, or 7pm. Seven o'clock came and went with no news of the aircraft. George Fleming and I put our feet up in his office where our dinner consisted of a couple of cheese sandwiches and a cup of tea. I remember him and me watching black and white television on a small set he had in his office - the sole concession to help pass the endless hours of waiting. It was actually fascinating to watch Real Madrid play the kind of football we could only dream about.

We went through the standard routines of both trying to telephone Overseas Aviation's operation desk at Gatwick Airport and sending innumerable telexes, knowing full well that we were wasting our time. Every hour or so I would make a passenger announcement on the airport Tannoy system to the effect the flight was delayed due to 'technical' reasons - whatever that meant. The airline had two further flights scheduled for that evening, one was for Arrowsmiths of Liverpool destined for Rimini, on the Italian Adriatic, and the second, if I recall correctly, was a Suntours charter to Valencia.

So, by midnight, three lots of passengers were backed up at the Airport and understandably tempers were once again becoming frayed. At eleven o'clock I was summoned back to the check-in desk to confront a very angry client. Without saying a word he handed me his business card: I can't remember his Christian name but he was a Mr Henry of the Manchester Evening News. I thought for a moment he wanted to interview me but then he said, 'Now you know who I am perhaps you wouldn't mind telling me what has happened to our flight?' All very polite, but it wasn't going to get him any information; I could hardly give him what I didn't possess.

'I really don't know. We've been trying all evening to find out where the aircraft is located, but, I'm sorry, we just don't have any news.'

'When are you likely to know?' I remember shrugging my shoulders. 'I wish I knew, Mr Henry. We're doing the best we can and as soon as we have some information we'll let you know.' He walked away, or perhaps sailed, would be more appropriate, disdainfully. At midnight I made a further announcement about technical problems, and once again at one o'clock in the morning. By then, George was snoring in his office, which I found irritating so I wandered down to the Operations Room to check whether there was anything on the telex. Fortuitously, a message came in about half an hour later from Gatwick control to the effect that Papa Foxtrot; an Overseas Aviation Argonaut had just taken off for Manchester. 'Thank Christ for that', I said aloud. Just then George wandered into the room and glanced at the message.

'It's not your flight.'

'What do you mean, it's not our flight?' He checked his flight schedules.

'Papa Foxtrot is scheduled to do the Valencia sector for Suntours. Sorry.' I gave it some quick thought and then took George to one side. 'George,' I said earnestly, 'the only people who know that are you and me and the crew. That's right, isn't it?' He looked at me suspiciously.

'What are trying to say, Vincent?'

'Change the bloody schedule is what I'm saying. Tell the crew there's been a change of flight plan; instead of doing Valencia, they're now operating the Palma route. Why the hell should they care anyway?'

'And what about Suntours?'

'Come off it, George. Their flight is scheduled way behind ours, and we're already six hours down so we've got to be first in the queue. Anyway, they don't have a rep. here so how are they going to know?' He sighed heavily, but he took the point.

'Ok. I'll let the crew know when they land. I'll check with the tower what time it's due in, then we'll schedule departure an hour after that. But...' he pointed a finger at me, 'you owe me. Just remember that.'

God! What a relief. The aircraft touched down on schedule and thirty minutes later we were calling the flight to the resounding cheers of the passengers. At precisely 0300 hours we taxied out to the runway, revved up the engines, while the checks were completed, then the brakes came off and we were quickly airborne. Unfortunately not for long! Twenty minutes or so into the flight, number four engine started spluttering, and then emitting flames. I got the inevitable call to the flight deck just as the aircraft banked to the left and started a hasty descent. 'We have a problem,' the pilot informed me, unnecessarily, I thought, I can see that.

'Are we returning to Ringway?'

'Yes. It's our nearest airport. I've alerted the emergency services that we'll be touching down in about ten minutes. But I have to tell you, I've feathered the engine but so far we haven't been able to extinguish the fire. I've also started to dump some fuel but we'll still be landing with a hell of a lot of weight. Do you think you can help with the passengers?'

'What? You mean stop them from panicking? Isn't that the stewardesses' job?' 'Normally, yes. But these two have had a series of misfortunes of late and they could do with some help. Do you mind?'

'I'll see what I can do.' Actually I didn't have a bloody clue. I mean I wasn't exactly diplomatic and I had immediate visions of Mr Henry handing me another business card just before he fainted! I went back into the cabin as the co-pilot was making the announcement about returning to Manchester. The problem was that the passengers on the port side (the left side) of the plane could see the flames shooting out of number four-engine. Many of them began stifling sobs, which in turn quickly transformed into screams. The stewardesses did their best but they didn't exactly

look confident, with their pale faces and tense
expressions. As I went down the aisle trying to
reassure passengers there was nothing to worry
about, one of the ladies on board asked me what
they should do. I remembered a comment I'd
heard from one of those hard guys in a recent film,
so I leaned over and whispered: 'You could try
praying.' Believe it or not, she began laughing. At
first I thought it was hysteria but in fact she was
genuinely amused and it did help her. Anyway, it
didn't last long We were soon on the approach
path and I could see the fire engines lining up,
followed quite closely by the ambulances. It was
quite dramatic, but was ultimately a non- event,
because we landed safely and the fire brigade
doused the flames from the engine as we hurtled
along the runway, stopping just before we ran out
of tarmac. Then it was a helter skelter down the
chutes, in what I considered to be a normal
disorderly disembarkation, the only minor
casualty being a sprained ankle. I watched the
ground staff preparing to tow away the Argonaut
(it was rather sad, I thought) as I joined the bus
with the rest of the passengers to return to the
transit terminal, whereupon I was surrounded by
a group of them wanting to know what would
happen next. I could only shrug, noncommittally -
there was really nothing I could tell them, which
by then, I was coming to realise was the story of
my travel life so far. However, I was able to
promise them we would move out of the transit

lounge as soon as I had cleared it with immigration. The next thing I did was to go and look for George Fleming to check whether or not he had some information. I just managed to catch him on the point of doing a runner. 'I've had enough,' he told me. 'There's no point in hanging around here; I can't get any information, there's no sign of any aircraft, and I haven't been paid now for the last two months. This bloody airline is on its last legs.'

'Hey, hang on, George,' I protested. 'You can't just push off like this. There are over two hundred passengers in the terminal waiting to fly off on holiday. You can't leave them in the shit. You have a responsibility to them.'

'Like hell I do,' he said angrily. 'They're not going to pay my wages, are they? And anyway, you and your passengers have just had first hand experience of the state the planes are in. You're all bloody lucky to be alive. The best thing you can do is tell them their holiday is cancelled, so they may as well go on home.'

'For Christ's sake, George,' I snapped, 'get a grip on yourself, will you. All we've had is an emergency landing, and we both know there's nothing either unusual or particularly alarming about that. It's certainly not the end of the bloody world. And anyway, I don't know what you're going on about, it was me on the flight not you. Look,' I said, trying to calm him down, 'why don't we go back to the Ops Room and see if they have any news on the other aircraft due in? Ours isn't the only flight scheduled for tonight. Last night. Sorry? The flights were scheduled for last night. It's now five o'clock on Saturday morning. And I'm knackered!' He thought about it for a moment then gave me one of his customary grins. 'Come on then. I don't suppose another hour or two will make any difference.' I breathed a sigh of relief and followed him down towards the Ops Room where a telex message was waiting. Evidently an Overseas Aviation Argonaut had just taken off from Gatwick with a full load of passengers bound for Malaga. Its schedule was Gatwick/Malaga/Manchester/Palma: it was our aircraft! I felt as if I had won the pools. This meant a flight of approximately five hours to Malaga; an hour on the ground refuelling, then a return flight to Manchester of, let's say, six hours. So it should land in Ringway at around six o'clock this evening. Give it a bit of time for servicing and we could be talking about a Palma take off at about eight o'clock.

At least I had something to tell the passengers, but how they would react was anyone's guess. By then they would be into a twenty-five hour delay; lengthy even by current standards. But at least George had promised to hang on for a while. Then I thought: 'What would Norman do?' One thing was for sure, he wouldn't tell them they had to wait around in a crappy airport lounge for the next fifteen hours. So I invited them to take refreshments on the company, explaining that I would have more news for them in the next couple of hours, which in itself was a bloody silly idea because there was nowhere open at that hour. I beat a hasty retreat before anyone could physically attack me. At seven o'clock in the morning, I too had had enough. More than twenty of the clients had already decided to cancel on the spot. So I rang Norman (long distance!) and got him out of bed, explaining the problem to him. 'What do you expect me to do?' he asked irritably. 'I'm sixty miles away, and you've woken me up.' Which I thought was just a little insensitive given that I hadn't had any sleep since Thursday. 'Norman, I need some help here,' I pleaded, 'These people are going to lynch me unless we do something. We can't leave them in the airport lounge until eight tonight. It's already like a cattle pen here, and it's going to get a damn sight worse during the day when all the other flights are delayed, including our Malaga flight I might add.' 'Oh, Christ!' he complained. 'I suppose I'd better come over, but you'll have to give me a couple of hours. Look, Vincent, why don't you get hold of that Manchester coach company, you know, the one we used last week to take those clients back to Liverpool?'

'Right. Then what?'

'Then we take them on an excursion for the day. Up to Buxton. It's nice up there in the summer. Give them lunch - not an expensive one, enough to keep them happy. 'They can have a look round the town, then have a rest in the afternoon, and we'll bring them back to Ringway for about five o'clock. That should do the trick.'

'Okay. But what do I tell them about the delay? And what do I do for money?'

'Bloody hell, do I have to do all your thinking for you? Tell them we're organising another plane, which is true anyway, and we should be departing about lunchtime. They won't complain about that. I'll bring some cash with me - see you shortly.' And that is exactly what we did. The coach company was more than happy to oblige, the passengers were reluctantly agreeable and an hour later they were on their way, with private instructions from myself to the driver about the arrangements when they got to Buxton.

I grabbed George, who was talking with Bernard Johnson, the Operations Manager of Starways Aviation, the Liverpool based airline, and we headed off to the staff canteen for some breakfast and a respite. Bernard, because of his ulcers, settled for his customary bottle of milk. Norman finally turned up at ten o'clock, cheerful and full of his usual charm, telling me I worried too much and if I weren't careful I would end up like Bernard Johnson with ulcers. Then he disappeared for half an hour or so, returning with the suggestion that he would now take care of the Malaga passengers. I genuinely thought he was going to recommend that I get some much needed rest - but then that would be totally out of character. I was right. He informed me that he had arranged for me to hitch a ride on a Bristol Wayfarer (an old type of aircraft now converted to ferry cars across the Channel) to Gatwick. His idea was that once there I could try and chase up Overseas Aviation Operations for information on what was happening to our flight to Malaga. He refused to accept George's word that there was no one there. 'You'll find someone,' he said, waving a hand dismissively. And in a way he was right.

After an hour in what was probably the noisiest and most uncomfortable aircraft in service, I landed at Gatwick only to discover it was true, the offices were closed, but eventually I was able to get hold of the home address of one of the company's directors from an airport rep. He lived in Crawley, literally five minutes away. I grabbed a taxi and a little while later I was knocking on his door. I then spent the next ten minutes or so publicly rowing on his doorstep before I was able to convince him - after threatening him with the press - to come back to the airport with me. By now it was two o'clock in the afternoon.

He opened the offices and we spent the next two hours on the telexes trying to locate the 'missing' Argonauts. I was beginning to get worried because the passengers on the Palma flight were due to be returning by now from

Buxton. Christ only knew what Norman had done with the Malaga Passengers. What a bloody mess! We still had no information when one of the guys from Airport Ops stuck his head round the door to inform us that an Argonaut was on finals and would be touching down in two minutes. The director contacted the tower and they confirmed it was coming in from Barcelona with a full load. However, it was scheduled to turn straight round and board a group of passengers from Riviera Holidays destined for Palma. 'It bloody well is not,' I told him, after learning it was only four hours or so down on its original schedule. 'We have passengers in Manchester who have been delayed now for over nineteen hours and still counting. So I want that aircraft, to hell with the Riviera lot!' 'And how am I supposed to do that?' he sneered. I glared at him face to face.

'Simple. You inform the new aircrew that they are now positioning the plane to Manchester and that from there they will fly Gaytours' passengers to Palma and then return with our inbound group to Manchester. And I'll tell you what we're going to do if you don't agree: we'll fly our remaining passengers, who are stuck in Manchester, to Gatwick by scheduled service, with instructions that they, and the media, park outside either your office here or your home, until you find them the aircraft they have paid for. Now, if you think I'm kidding, then let me tell you I am thoroughly pissed off, I've had no proper sleep since Thursday and it would give me immense pleasure to blast you and your bloody disgraceful airline across the front pages of the nationals. So why don't you give me the opportunity?'

'You're an arrogant young bastard, aren't you? But I take your point' he added, holding up his arms in a kind of symbolic surrender, 'Why don't you go and get a sandwich or something and I'll see what I can do. Give me about an hour.' He was as good as his word. Just over an hour later he confirmed that the aircraft would be taking off for Manchester at 5 pm local time to operate the delayed flight to Palma. I would be travelling on it. We got a telex message off to Ringway Ops confirming the new arrangements and by five thirty I was in the air and sharing a cup of coffee with a couple of bright and breezy stewardesses. We landed on schedule at approximately six o'clock with a provisional take off time to Palma of 1930 hours, or 7.30 pm. Everything was going well for a change; the aircraft was being re fuelled, the passengers had been informed following their excursion to Buxton and Norman had long departed for God knows where, leaving me to deal not only with this flight but also the Malaga charter. It turned out that his idea of taking care of the Malaga passengers was to send them by coach to Tatton Park, a Stately Home near Knutsford in Cheshire! The bad news was that they were due back any time and there was no sign whatsoever of the aircraft for their flight.

The only news we had was a cryptic telex from Malaga Airport to the effect that our plane was delayed 'indefinitely'. The only thing we could hope for was that somehow we would be able to retain the plane I had 'commandeered' from Gatwick and try to arrange for a crew to fly it to Malaga on its return from Palma. That would be at the earliest ten hours from now, or five o'clock in the morning. And I had been given the lousy job of having to tell them. What was it someone had once said? 'Have you ever had the feeling that things are so bad they couldn't possibly get any worse? And then they do!'

That is precisely how things now began to develop. As I still had important business to carry out in Majorca, it was decided that I would continue on the flight and George Fleming would not only look after the Malaga group but also endeavour to find an aircraft for them. Then, half an hour prior to take off for Palma I received a call from the Captain, who wanted to see me. The flight had already been called and the relieved passengers were going through immigration and into the departure lounge. 'We have a problem,' he informed me – God! I was so sick of that statement! He was a big man with an even bigger moustache; a former squadron leader in the RAF during the Second World War. He looked at me intensely as if somehow the problem, whatever it might be, was my responsibility. 'So what is it this time?' I asked him dryly. 'Something really trivial, like one of the engines has fallen off? Or the undercarriage is stuck?'

'You have obviously flown with us before,' he commented dryly. 'Actually, it isn't too serious. We've just lost our back up 'mag' and there's no way we can fly without one.' 'I don't know what that means?' I admitted, 'and I don't really care. All I'm bothered about is how long before you can fix it?'

'Well, fortunately, the engineers can cannibalise a spare from Papa Foxtrot - the Argonaut you emergency landed in a few hours ago. It's over by the cargo shed and they've already started working on it. We should be able to complete the repairs in a couple of hours. But someone will have to inform the passengers.' I remember sighing wearily and wondering if either the passengers or I would ever get away from this bloody airport. We were now into a twenty-four hour delay and when the captain lightly referred to a further two hours I could only react cynically. I walked back to the departure lounge wondering what was I going to tell them? By now they were sick and tired of excuses, apart from which we had run out of the plausible ones, so I decided I would tell them the truth. There was the inevitable shocked silence when I had finished but six or seven clients picked up their hand baggage and, without speaking, left the lounge. I followed in their wake to try to reason with them but they were beyond listening. 'What about your suitcases?' I asked. 'They're already on board the plane.' An elderly lady, her face showing all the strain she had endured throughout the past twenty-four hours, stopped to answer the question. 'Right now, young man, I care more about my life and my sanity than I do about a couple of suitcases.' She waved her hand towards the other departing passengers. 'We are all weary, and frankly we have had enough. If you ever do get to Majorca and you come across the cases - our names and addresses are on the labels - perhaps you would be kind enough to see that they are returned to us.' She turned and walked away, leaving me feeling more than a little ashamed of this industry of ours. And I certainly couldn't blame her or the other passengers for admitting defeat.

We finally took off at midnight with only forty-eight of the original seventy-three passengers on board: twenty-five cancellations. It was pitch black with just a few stars piercing the cloud cover. In the condition I was in it was hard to remember when I had last seen any real daylight. I sat on my own at the rear of the plane smoking what must have been my sixtieth cigarette since I had arrived at the airport. The passengers had been given something to eat at the airport (Readymade sandwiches I was later told) so the cabin staff was serving only coffee and light refreshments. I ate very little in those days; I never seemed to have the time and anyway I preferred a cigarette to a meal. Probably that would explain why I weighed a mere ten and a half stone. One of the stewardesses came to join me, very kindly bringing me a cup of that undrinkable airline coffee. Her name was Bridgette. She was a pleasant girl, about the same age as me, and she told me that this was her first year in the job. 'What do you think the chances are of getting to Palma?' I asked her. 'Oh, we'll be fine,' she assured me. 'Captain Baines knows what he's doing he's a very good pilot.'

'I wasn't asking about his flying skills, I'm more worried about the plane; they seem to have a reluctance to stay in the air!' She laughed, more I thought from the nervousness that comes from experience than amusement. 'I think I know what you mean. These planes are a bit unreliable, aren't they? Were you with these passengers on Papa Foxtrot?' I nodded.

'Do you think they're scared?' she asked.

'Some of them are bound to be, don't you think? I mean, apart from an emergency landing with an engine on fire and then having to slide down chutes, it's now thirty hours since they were due to take off - and we're not there yet. So they've already lost nearly two days of their holiday. If it were my holiday I'd be really pissed off, wouldn't you?' Instead of answering I noticed that she was peering towards the front of the cabin. Smoke was appearing from somewhere and was rapidly spreading throughout the passenger compartment. Then the seatbelt signs came on, followed by what I guessed must have been a warning hooter through the plane. 'You see to the passengers, Bridgette. I'll go and have a word with your Captain Baines. I reckon we must have tempted providence.'

'So talk to me, Captain,' I suggested when I reached the flight deck. He seemed to be calm enough, I thought. So it was possible we might not be in danger of crashing just yet.

'Yeah. These bloody old kites, they're always going wrong. We've got a problem with the pressurisation system. I've shut it down but it appears to have a mind of its own; I'm damned if we can stop the smoke.'

'How long before we all suffocate?' He looked at me quizzically.

'Jesus! You're not kidding, are you?'

'No. And neither would you be if you checked the state of the cabin. People are already having problems breathing.'

'Haven't the masks come down?'

'I haven't seen any. Mind you, it's difficult to see anything with all that smoke.'

'I'm dealing with it, Skipper,' the co-pilot said. 'The automatic release valve must be stuck. I'm trying to free it up by hand.'

'I don't care if you use your dick, just get it freed up we're running out of time.'

'Do you need a hand?' I proffered.

'Yeah. Thanks. Could you help me turn this nozzle anticlockwise? It's tightened up and I can't release it on my own.' It took some effort but after a few seconds it responded. I went aft to the cabin and saw, through the smoke, that the passengers each had a mask to their face breathing in oxygen. The two stewardesses were at the back also with a mask. Almost everyone looked scared to death.

I went back to the cockpit and said, 'Aren't you going to make an announcement?' I demanded of the Captain. 'You can't simply leave the passengers like this with oxygen masks round their mouths and no explanation as to what has gone wrong. Some of them are terrified - they've already had one emergency landing, remember.'

'Oh. Yeah, right. But you do know we're on our way back to Ringway, don't you?' 'Well I knew we weren't going to make it to Palma on this crate, and it wouldn't surprise me if the passengers had cottoned on either. But I believe they'll be more concerned about whether they'll get back alive or not, wouldn't you Skipper?' I laid heavy on the sarcasm at his title but he seemed totally unconcerned; probably came from dogfights with German Messerschmitt, I thought. 'And why Ringway? Isn't Gatwick the closer of the two?'

'It is, yes. But we can still use the parts on Papa Foxtrot if we return to Manchester. That could save us a lot of time.'

'Ladies and gentlemen,' the announcement began, 'this is the Captain speaking. I regret to inform you that we have experienced a problem with our pressurisation system and I would ask that you keep the oxygen masks held to your face. There is nothing to be alarmed about and the aircraft is perfectly safe but unfortunately it does mean we shall have to return to Manchester for repairs. Upon arrival at the airport, and purely as a matter of routine, we shall be making an emergency landing. I do appreciate you have recently undergone a similar experience, and I can only apologise on behalf of the company. At the same time, I would re-emphasise that this action is merely part of standard safety procedures and there is nothing whatsoever to worry about. The stewardesses will be there to help you and they will be able to answer any questions you may have. Thank you for your patience.' 'How was that?' he then asked me. 'Will it do the trick?' I laughed. 'I doubt it will convince them. In fact I suspect they'll be likening it to the Captain's announcement on the Titanic just before it went down!

'You weren't serious were you? About it being a matter of standard safety procedures?'

'Hell, no! But what was I supposed to say? We're still carrying a heavy load of fuel and it will take just one tiny spark and we'll all go up in flames? Anyway, no doubt they'll get the message when the stewardesses take them through the emergency landing procedures. As it is, I've been given priority - landing facilities. They're clearing the skies around the airport and emergency services have been alerted. We're twenty eight minutes from touchdown.'

'Clearing the skies?' I snorted. 'There's nothing to clear. All the bloody planes are kaput! But you've made your point, Captain, so I'll check on the passengers.'

CHAPTER NINE

THE LONG WEEKEND (Continued)

I wandered back to the cabin asking myself what it was that these old World War Two pilots flew exactly? I had the feeling they flew nothing larger than kites! This time a number of the passengers were genuinely suffering from shock. A few of the younger ladies were sobbing; their husbands were doing their best to comfort them but they weren't much better themselves. It was the older ones who were much more stoical. I went slowly along the aisle dishing out reassuring, and unconvincing, words of placation. 'Nothing to worry about.' 'Standard procedure.' 'We'll be down before you know it.' All the time wondering to myself exactly what 'down' might mean in this instance. By now it was becoming a familiar sight as we crossed the threshold lights: fire engines desperately trying to match our landing speed, ambulances hoping for the best and expecting the worst, police cars, lights flashing as if they were showing us the way, only there I suspected because they had nothing better to do. I didn't know which was the louder either, the engines thrusting against the drag of the flaps, or the commotion some of the passengers were making in the cabin. No one on the flight deck spoke, other than the Captain calling for 'brakes' as we touched down gently on the runway. It was a smooth landing and we stopped within the statutory distance. Once again we received the foam treatment from the fire engines as the passengers slid down the chutes. This time there was no panic, no screams, and no injuries. All very civilised and very matter of fact; you wouldn't believe that this was our second consecutive emergency landing in less than thirty-six hours. I stayed with the crew to wait for the Engineers to arrive and for the bowser to empty the fuel from the tanks. The chief was evidently still on duty and he grinned when he saw me. 'Not you again? Don't you know when to quit?'

'I was born inherently stupid,' I confessed.

'You can say that again! Okay, gang, let's have a look again at this old bird.'

We hung around for the next half hour or so until the chief reappeared at the top of the steps.

'Can it be repaired?' the Captain shouted against the background throb of the portable generators.

'It can if you're not in a hurry. I'm going to have to strip the cylinders out and replace some of the seals – that's where your smoke was coming from. You want to come up and have a look?' We all trudged up the steps as if we knew what we were talking about, and then nodded intelligently as the chief pointed out the various jobs he would have to carry out. Eventually I'd had enough of trying to be something I was not so I said, apropos of nothing, 'How long, Chief?' He scratched his chin thoughtfully. 'Well, I reckon if we tow her alongside Papa Foxtrot we can halve the time it would normally take. Let's say, to be on the safe side, four hours at the most.'

'Oh Christ!' was all I could think to say. 'Four hours! We'll have no passengers left.' He had a great sense of humour - he nearly killed himself laughing. 'I don't think it will be the length of the delay that'll discourage them from flying in this old kite again. Bloody hell, man, they've been through two emergency landings already; you don't think they'll risk a third, do you?' I shrugged. I mean, what else could I do? 'Well if they all cancel we'll just have to use this 'old kite' for the Malaga flight, won't we? At least that will solve one of the problems.' 'Yeah. Well. That isn't my concern. Come on guys, let's organise the tow.'

If the airport 'lounge' was like a cattle pen before, it was now more like the Stretford Road End at Old Trafford on match day. People were literally crammed almost like sardines in a tin. There were by now over five hundred passengers stranded in a space that would be crowded if it held two hundred. The Airport Police were going spare at the melee. One of the inspectors I knew informed me that they were seriously considering either erecting a marquee or even bussing passengers out to places such as Sale and Wythenshawe. In some ways it made my job a bit easier. There were that many people there, and that many delayed flights, not all of them, in fairness, belonging to Overseas Aviation, that our own passengers developed something of a sense of community within them, which diverted their attention away from their own plight.

The exception, as I expected, was Mr Henry. He approached me at the cheek in desk and handed me yet another business card. 'Thank you, sir,' was all I said. He glared at me. 'You do realise who I am, don't you?'

'I believe I do, Mr. Henry, particularly as you've now given me three of your business cards.'

'So?'

'So I still can't tell you what is happening to your plane!' 'You're going to regret this,' he said assertively, leaving me with the thought that I had been regretting it for the last couple of days! I found George eventually in the staff canteen with Bernard Johnson, who was still drinking his milk. 'Give me some good news, George,' I pleaded. He pointed towards Bernard. 'He's just got a flight away. And it's only down nine hours! That's got to be good news, hasn't it?'

'Lucky bugger. But there's no guarantee it won't be back again, is there?'

'God! You're becoming a right Job's comforter in your old age,' Bemard exclaimed. 'Do you really blame me?' I pointed in the general direction of the terminal. 'I've got two planeloads of passengers up there. The first lot have been delayed now for almost thirty-six hours and they'll still have to hang around for another two or three - that's if we're very lucky. And the second lot that Norman promised me he would take care of before he pissed off and left me with them, have no sign of an aircraft for the Malaga flight, and they've been delayed for ... Christ! I forget. How long is it, George?'

'Not too long. Only about twelve hours actually. And if you remember I have been giving your passengers the benefit of my very talented assistance. So there's no reason for you to be so bloody miserable, is there? Besides, it isn't true they don't have a plane. I'm reliably informed that there's an Argonaut Inbound at this very moment from Venice. It is, of course, scheduled for Global Tours but with your charm I'm sure you'll be able to persuade me to let you have it. Now if that doesn't cheer you up I don't know what will.' He grinned widely, like a mischievous schoolboy who's just played a naughty trick.

'Great. All we need now is to get the Palma plane back in service and we'll be laughing. How is it getting on, by the way, George?'

'Dunno. I haven't checked lately.'

'Well do you think you might make the effort?' I enquired disarmingly. 'I realise how knackered you must be but those passengers have been at this airport almost as long as we have and I do feel that they're entitled to some information. Or don't you agree?' He got up from his seat shaking his head. 'You're a bloody hard taskmaster, Vincent. I'll see what I can find out.' After he left, I noticed through the canteen windows that another day was breaking. There was still a heavy cloud cover but the watery late July sun was doing its best to struggle out of its grip. Bernard had gone off for yet some more milk. I sank my head into my arms across the table and crashed out. It felt as though I had only been asleep for a matter of minutes, but when I was woken by George; he assured me he had been gone for over two hours! 'What time is it?' I mumbled, trying to clear my head. 'Just gone seven. And your plane will be ready within the hour. Are you going to let your passengers know?'

'Am I hell! Last time I did that we had to offload them again. I'll inform them when that Captain Baines has actually started the engines and finished his pre take off checks.' I looked at my watch - it read seven twenty. 'So what do you reckon, George? Eight thirty take off?' He nodded his assurance. 'More or less. Oh, and the Venice charter is scheduled to arrive now at about ten so if you like I'll take care of your Malaga passengers in your absence.'

'Yeah. Thanks. Anything else happening?'

'Not really. Except I received a telex about an hour ago from Malaga that was a bit weird.'

'Oh? In what way?'

'I can't make it out tell you the truth. It was from Shell to the effect that they are refusing to refuel our aircraft on the ground at Malaga Airport unless we pay them some money. I didn't realise we owed them anything.'

'So it's stuck on the ground?'

'Sort of, yes. And I'm a bit worried about what will happen to your flight when it gets there unless London can sort it out quickly.'

'Have you tried to get hold of them?'

'Yes. I spoke with Patterson the guy you dragged out of his house. He assures me it's just a misunderstanding, but how often have we heard that before?'

'You think they're going bust, George, don't you?' He scowled as he took a seat next to me. 'I'd be a liar if I said I wasn't worried. I told you earlier I hadn't been paid for two months, didn't I? Well I've now heard they haven't paid any landing fees either for the last six weeks.' He shrugged philosophically. 'I don't suppose it matters much as long as people keep giving them credit; I just hope that the Shell telex isn't a warning shot across their bows.'

'Bloody hell, that's all we need. Still, there's not a damn thing we can do about it, is there? Except keep our fingers crossed.' The Tannoy system interrupted us with the announcement of the departure of the flight to Palma. I heard a loud cheer go up through the system. 'Here we go again. I'll see you in about, what? An hour?' George grinned again in his inimitable style. 'Have a safe flight,' he said.

'Piss off, George!' It was exactly eight thirty on the Sunday morning when the plane rose from the ground – thirty-seven and a half hours late. Our payload by now was down to a mere twenty-four passengers; a total of forty-nine passengers had cancelled, including Mr Henry and his family. I wondered if it was some kind of a record. The other thought I had was what happening to the inbound passengers? There were over sixty of them stuck God knows where. It was impossible to contact our rep by phone as there was an interminable delay on the International exchange; it was almost impossible to even get through to the operator. I thought about sending of a telex through the airport's facilities but I doubted this would even reach the reps. Christ, what a mess.

Finally, Captain Baines had assured me that the pressurisation unit was sorted out and that we could now expect a trouble free flight. I remained quiet at that; I'd had enough of tempting providence. So I took my customary seat at the rear of the plane and promptly fell asleep again - I didn't even bother with a smoke.

The noise of people shouting disturbed me and then someone was shaking my shoulder. It was one of the stewardesses. 'Don't tell me,' I groaned. 'We have a problem. What is it this time?'

'Captain Baines wants you up front, Vincent. Apparently number two engine has gone. We're having to go back.' 'Oh shit! These poor people are destined not to have a holiday.'

'No. You don't understand. We're in serious trouble.' I virtually ran up to the flight deck. How much more trouble could there possibly be? I asked myself. 'Now what?' 'I've had to feather number two,' the Captain said. 'But now number four is on the blink - and we have a flame out. We're heading back, I'm afraid. And we're going to have to try a landing on only two engines.'

'Are we going back to Ringway?'

'No. Gatwick is the nearest emergency airport. But I don't think we'll be going anywhere after that - this old bird has had her day.'

'Yeah. So have these passengers.' I hesitated for a moment. 'Are we going to make it?' I then asked him. He seemed to have aged in a matter of hours. His face turned towards me; it was drained of colour and it was then that I started to fear the worst. The First Officer was already struggling with the controls as if he were riding an untamed horse. I could see the veins of his hands protruding with the strain, like pieces of taut purple string. The Captain still hadn't answered my question but then he didn't need to; his face told its own story. My own mind was in a whirl and it was an odd phenomenon but I noticed through the windscreen of the aircraft that it was now raining heavily. 'What do we say to the passengers?' I asked when my head cleared a little. 'Without causing a panic,' I added quickly.

'One things for sure, I can't make the same announcement as last time. Apart from it not being the truth, they wouldn't believe it anyway. Have you any ideas?'

'How about if we tell them we're about to crash and although we can't promise not to kill anyone, we'll do our level best?'

'That was in very poor taste...' He was about to continue when the plane suddenly lurched violently to starboard throwing me across the flight deck and on to the floor, splitting my lip. 'Bloody hell, Captain,' I muttered, 'It wasn't that insensitive.' He didn't speak for a while; both he and his co-pilot were far too busy fighting with the controls. When the plane stabilised somewhat he turned and handed me the mike for the intercom. 'Here. They're your passengers, you make the Announcement.' I thought about it for a moment, and then said aloud, 'Oh, sod it!' and depressed the button. 'Ladies and gentlemen, my name is Vincent Cobb and I am the Manager of Gaytours, your tour company. Unfortunately, as by now you will be aware, we are experiencing difficulties with two of the engines, which mean in effect that we are having to divert to Gatwick Airport to make an emergency landing.

'Now, I apologise for this inconvenience and I do appreciate you have all had a bad time of it. But, and I want you to consider this, we are all in this situation together and if we help each other I'm sure we can come through it safely. So I would ask you to please remain calm, listen to the stewardesses, they are very experienced in these matters, and everything should be all right. I will be passing down the cabin and I will answer any questions you may have for me. In the meantime, I would ask you to fasten your seat belts, place your seats in an upright position, and extinguish your cigarettes. Thank you for your attention.'

'Very good,' said the Captain. 'We should offer you a job.'

'I'll be happy to turn it down if we survive this disaster. Good luck, you two. Don't give up the faith.' I passed along the cabin, stopping to speak with a number of the distraught passengers but it was a futile effort. If I described them as scared the previous time this had happened there were simply no words to convey the state they were in now - other perhaps than terrified. One or two were throwing up, a few of them burst into tears, while others sat there tight-lipped under the strain. A couple of the men tried to get up from their seats as if they could somehow jump safely from the rapidly descending plane. With the help of one of the stewardesses, Bridgette, I believe it was, we forced them back into their seats and fastened their belts. As for myself, I was still a practising Catholic in those days, albeit not a very devout one; in fact I used to argue that I was using condoms when the Vatican still believed they were party balloons! And no matter how hard

I tried I just couldn't reduce myself to the level of hypocrisy by saying a silent prayer.

As it happens I had never thought I would live very long - my father had died suddenly when he was only forty-three and I assumed that it ran in the family. So, although I wasn't exactly indifferent to the crisis we were facing - a thread of something close to fear was running through me - I did my best to remain composed and fatalistic. Besides, I thought, someone had to keep a sense of objectivity. On the advice of Captain Baines I went to the rear of the aircraft and positioned myself by the exit door. I noticed that there was an axe bracketed on to the door, so I removed it and placed it by my side just in case. From the window in the door I could now faintly make out the distant lights of Gatwick Airport. We were probably some ten or twelve minutes from touchdown. Next, I heard the sound of the undercarriage at the same time as the flaps were lowered to seventy-five degrees. Less than five minutes now to touchdown. It was at that moment that the number two engine flared and triggered off screams as the passengers witnessed the flames pouring out. In turn the hubbub provoked an immediate panic. A number of them fought their way out of their seats, sadly I have to say, they were mostly men, and came towards me at the rear of the plane. I lifted the axe in a threatening gesture and glared at them. 'Where the hell do you think you're going?' I shouted.

'We've got to get out, we're going to die,' one man said in a panic. 'Get out of the way.' He then raised a fist at me as if to throw a punch. I pushed him back against the others, and said, as menacingly as I could, 'If you come any closer I'm going to split your skulls open. I'm serious,' I said, taking a step towards them. Evidently the prospect of a split skull was much more immediate than a crash landing because they all backed off. I took another step towards them this time raising the axe even higher and in a fairly calm voice I said: 'You're not the heroes who fought in the last war, are you? God! If your families could see you now. Go on, get back to your seats, you should be ashamed of yourselves.' It did the trick. They turned and slouched back like a bunch of recalcitrant puppies that had just been admonished. I gave a big sigh of relief and placed the axe back in its holder. It wouldn't be needed anymore; not unless it was for the purpose for which it was originally intended. I strapped myself into one of the crew seats next to the stewardesses. 'Sorry about that,' I whispered over the noise of the engines. Bridgette took hold of my hand and began squeezing the blood out of it. The other girl was sitting there white faced, a tear in the corner of her eye and her lips trembling. I reached across Bridgette and took hold of her hand, smiling to let her know it would be okay. Jesus! I must have been some kind of an optimist. I could see the smoke and flames coming out of the engine even from where we were sitting. Then I saw the runway lights beneath us. Shit or bust, I thought, clenching my teeth. It's too late now anyway.

I was asked later how I would describe the landing. I said it was the most miraculous piece of flying I had ever or would ever experience. The touchdown felt more like settling in a soft pudding than the hard tarmac. We were informed later that the fire authorities had foamed the runway to reduce the risk of an explosion from the engine. Admittedly we skidded and spun along in a somewhat macabre dance; admittedly, some passengers were screaming in sheer terror, especially when our vision through the windows was obliterated by the spume of foam being thrown at us from both sides of the aircraft, and admittedly 'Someone' up there must have liked us, but you could take nothing away from the crew and I include the stewardesses in this. They were absolutely brilliant. We came to a stop at the very end of the runway. I will always remember the stillness that seemed to settle over us. It was as if the passengers had suddenly become paralysed, whether it was with fear or not, I don't know, but the stewardesses and myself almost had to force them out of their seats and, once again head for the chutes. Before I left the plane I made a point of going onto the flight deck to shake the hands of the crew. The First Officer was wiping his brow; the Captain had completely regained his composure. 'How about that for a piece of flying?' I said. 'Absolutely bloody marvellous!'

'You're welcome,' he said. 'What are you going to do with the passengers?'

'Try and get them back to Manchester somehow. I don't think they'll be too keen on flying with Overseas Aviation again, do you?'

'They won't have to,' he said cryptically. 'Or to put it more accurately, they won't be able to.'

I looked at him puzzled. 'How do you mean?'

'I've just received a message from Ops. As of 1000 hours today we are now officially bankrupt! The only Overseas planes in the air are those returning to base with stranded passengers that's assuming there are any aircraft serviceable.'

'I'm sorry,' was all I could say. 'For all of us actually. I only hope things will get better in the future.'

Understandably some of the passengers were in a state of shock after the experience, and were taken away by ambulance for treatment. Many of the others had a dazed expression on their faces as if they were unsure whether to be grateful to be alive or whether the Grim Reaper might still be calling on them. Nevertheless, it was a miracle that no one had been seriously injured and I don't believe anyone could ever explain how we had avoided fatalities.

Now I was faced with the problem of arranging transport to Manchester Airport for what remained of the group. Flying was out of the question for all the obvious reasons, not least of which was the cost. A train journey was also going to be difficult: one, I didn't have sufficient money with me, and two, the passengers would have been deposited in the centre of the city when they all wanted to return to the airport. So the only answer left was the coach. Fortunately, we were in daylight hours so it didn't prove too difficult, but it did take me some time to get through to Norman to let him know what was happening and for him to convince the coach company we were good for the money. The news of Overseas Aviation's bankruptcy was already spreading throughout the industry and every company involved in transport was naturally afraid of the knock on effect to tour operators. So credit facilities had tightened considerably. Norman told me he would leave immediately for Manchester Airport to see what had happened to the Malaga passengers. I set off in the coach with a group of silent clients for the same destination, arriving after a journey of just over four hours.

As the clients were leaving the coach, one lady made a point of coming over to shake my hand: 'I wasn't able to say anything earlier,' she said, 'I was in too much shock. But I do think we owe you a vote of thanks; if you hadn't kept your head God knows what might have happened, the way some people were panicking.'

Somehow, that seemed to make all the stress worthwhile, and I returned her thanks. I met up with my boss at four that afternoon to discover that the Malaga passengers had mostly dispersed after the announcement was made on the loud speakers regarding the compulsory liquidation of the airline. George Fleming was still there; I suspected that he was hoping that we could give him a job, which wasn't a bad idea actually. In the meantime Norman had booked calls to Aviaco, the charter subsidiary of Iberia, the Spanish national carrier; he was also trying to contact any other airline he could to arrange for our passengers still stranded in Palma and Malaga to be returned home. We were both at the airport for the rest of the afternoon and evening doing our best to salvage something from the disaster. Finally, we received confirmation that Aviaco would depart from Palma at 2200 hours that night with the returning group and, after discussions with other tour operators similarly affected by the bankruptcy, we divided our Malaga passengers across two or three different flights. They would return during the night and into tomorrow. We didn't dare leave the airport until we had confirmation in our hands that the Aviaco flight had actually taken off from Palma. We breathed a sigh of relief when confirmation came through.

We managed to get away just before midnight on the Sunday, leaving in separate cars. By the time I arrived home almost seventy-two hours had passed since I had last seen a bed. There was one final small twist to the story of the 'Long

Weekend.' I had just gone through the village of Kirkham on the Preston/Blackpool road when I began to hallucinate; I was seeing lorries coming at me out of the darkness, forcing me once to mount the kerb at over sixty miles an hour. I daren't go any further so I pulled to the side of the road, leaned my head against the steering wheel, and promptly fell asleep. It was daylight when the police opened the driver's door to ask me if I was all right.

By the time I arrived home it was too late to go to bed, not so much because I couldn't have slept all day had I wished but because I had remembered that we had sent a cheque for seven thousand pounds on the previous Thursday to the Jersey Office of Overseas Aviation. The payment was in fact for all of the July flights. One of the things Norman was insistent upon in that climate was, unlike some of the other tour operators, only to pay for flights in arrears, never in advance. There was no way it could have cleared yet, so I waited in the office until precisely nine am when I rang our bank and cancelled the cheque. It was a major victory and one that allowed us to continue trading for the rest of the season even though ultimately we had to pay excessive prices for substitute charters. The airline's Jersey Bank, however, informed us that they had already given Overseas Aviation a special clearance on the cheque without waiting for clearance from our bank and claimed it was our responsibility to meet the amount. Naturally we declined and we never heard another word. Effectively we became an unsecured debtor of the bankrupt airline, but no claims were ever made against us.

CHAPTER TEN

1961 LATE SUMMER CAPTAIN BILKO

Following the debacle with Overseas Aviation we found ourselves, at the height of the season, with healthy passenger numbers but no aircraft. It became a scramble amongst most of the tour operators to charter flights from wherever they were available. I spent most of the summer flying across Europe; to Belgium to negotiate with Sabena, the national carrier, that we knew were re equipping with fanjets; to Rome for discussions with SAM, the charter subsidiary of Alitalia, and then to Madrid, where I found Aviaco, the subsidiary of Iberia, to be incredibly helpful. It was suggested that it was because my Spanish had improved to the point where I was able to converse with them, but whatever the reason, whenever they had a spare slot they let us have priority. Personally, I thought it was because they found my accent hilarious.

At the time there was no such thing as 'open skies'. Rather, we were all of us restricted by what was known then as 'Fifth Freedom Rights', which effectively meant that a foreign airline was able only to operate between the UK and the country of its origin. In other words, if we wished to charter a Sabena flight we would only be allowed to fly between say Manchester and a Belgian airport, or alternatively, it was possible to fly for instance between Manchester and Spain with Sabena, but you would have to have a stop in Brussels en route. On more than one occasion, in desperation, we were forced to do this.

On the 11th August our second daughter was born. My wife, unfortunately, had a very bad time with the birth and to make matters worse I was stuck in Jersey, fog bound at the time, consequently missing the occasion. To say the least, I was not very popular. And because of the ongoing pressures it was impossible for me, short of packing in the job, to find time for my family. It was two days after the British Eagle Viking came down in Stavanger, killing everyone on board, including thirty-four students. It was a sad day for the Tourist Industry.

I remember one instance, around the third week in August, I was in London late one Friday afternoon still trying to find an aircraft for the following day to operate the Palma and Malaga return legs: that is, we needed a plane to take passengers out to Palma, return empty to Manchester, and then take our group to Malaga and return with the inbound passengers. The broker with whom I was negotiating finally managed to find an old DC4 (were there any new ones?) belonging to an airline registered in Luxembourg called Seven Seas Aviation. As events transpired it turned out to be a one aircraft airline, owned and piloted by an American. Anyway, we settled on a schedule, not just for the flying, but also for the method of payment. The idea was that I would travel on the aircraft with the pilot, and when we arrived in Palma I would pay him cash for only that sector. When he arrived back in Manchester with me on board, Norman would pay him, again in cash, for the empty sector. Then we would change round and Norman would fly with him to Malaga and pay him for that leg and I would be waiting at Manchester Airport to pay him for the return. It was incredibly complicated but there was no way we were going to pay a cowboy outfit money in advance.

As circumstances later proved, it was a very sensible decision. I signed the contract, and then got a message off to Norman informing him of the schedules. They weren't too bad actually, providing you considered a departure eight hours later than the originally timetabled acceptable, and that you understood that it was impossible at this late stage to advise passengers of the change! But it was a contract and better than what we had, which was precisely nothing. And, would you believe, it meant that I again travelled from Gatwick Airport back to Blackpool on the overnight train!

Departure on the Saturday was therefore put back from the original time of 1100 hours to 1900 hours or seven pm. Norman and I travelled to

Manchester in separate cars; the reason being that I had to be there by about ten am to inform the passengers checking in about the delay. Norman would arrive later in the day with the boot of his own car stuffed full of cash. I had already been given the amount we were due to pay the pilot in Palma Airport and it was burning a hole in my pocket.

I won't bore you yet again with the reactions of the clients when they received the news; let me just say that it was fairly predictable and I was lucky to escape in one piece. The real problems began from six o'clock onwards when the aircraft failed to arrive. There was literally no information about its whereabouts or where it was coming from and neither was there an office for us to contact. So we all just sat there fuming, and then worrying about what we would do if he failed to turn up at all. I left Norman to do the really skilful work, which was trying to placate the passengers, while I spent the time in the Operations Room desperately attempting to glean some information; all to no avail. Norman was particularly furious because we had to provide the passengers with lunch and it had by now stretched into dinner both meals consisting of nothing more than salad and sandwiches! One of the stories the Airport Rep told to me was that when one of the passengers aggressively turned on Norman to complain he retorted, in typical fashion: 'The trouble with you people is that you have Rolls Royce appetites and tramcar budgets.'

I had heard him use the phrase before but not directly to the passengers; and I thought I was the one lacking in diplomacy! By now it was ten o'clock at night and getting dark. We were on the point of seriously deciding to cancel the flight when one of the Ops. Clerks came into the departure lounge, a grin all over his face. 'Your aircraft has just landed,' he smirked 'What's so funny?' Norman asked him 'Wait 'till you see the bloody thing. It's tied together with string.'

We wandered out to the apron for a look and watched this dilapidated old DC4 taxiing towards us' 'Good God!' Norman exclaimed. 'You wouldn't catch me in that thing.'

'I see. But it's okay if I go up in it? And those other poor buggers who've paid for a holiday?'

'Yes. Quite. But you know what I mean.' Then the pilot emerged - he was even funnier than his aeroplane. He was the double of Sergeant Bilko from the American TV series, not only in the way he looked, with the glasses perched on his nose, but also in the way he walked, with feet splayed outwards like a duck out of water. Even Norman started giggling and had to turn away.

'Hi,' he said in a broad American accent. 'Are you the guys from the tour company?' We shook hands with him and introduced ourselves. 'You're a bit on the late side,' Norman said. 'Yeah? Well, I got held up for a time in Toronto. I was only scheduled (he pronounced it skeduled!) to drop off an engine, but they insisted on examining the damn thing before I could leave. Anyway guys, here I am and raring to go. I just gotta file a flight plan, pay for the fuel, and then we'll be off. Where's this airport we're heading for? Palma de Mallorca isn't it?' I nodded, and asked him if he thought he could find it in the dark! He didn't see the funny side of that and proceeded to give me a lecture on navigation, and beacons. I still wasn't convinced, but then he had come all the way from Toronto to England and he had managed to find Manchester, which couldn't have been easy for a Yank. As he left for Flight Ops. I noticed Mac, the chief engineer waving at me. He and I had become quite pally in recent weeks; that's because I was spending as much time on the apron as I was in the terminal. 'Where do you find these fucking old crates, Vincent?'

'Desperation land,' I informed him cryptically. 'You know, that's the place where you go when you've run out of options. Why? What's wrong with it?'

'What's wrong with it?' he repeated. 'Well, if I had the authority I'd ground the bastard. Just look at this engine its leaking oil like a barrel with a hole in it. And if you want any more proof, go and have a look at the interior; about a third of the seats have no seatbelts, and nine or ten of them are broken. It's a cargo plane for Christ's sake. You can't put passengers in that.'

'I'll have a look, Mac, but we really have no choice.' I said wearily. 'You know as well as I do what a state the industry is in. And anyway, the question surely is, is it airworthy?' He shrugged. 'I guess. But I would still like to have a closer look at that engine; I agree, the industry is in a hell of a state but I wouldn't want to be responsible for making it worse.'

'Ask Captain Bilko about it. Perhaps there's a simple answer.'

'Who's Captain Bilko?'

'The American Pilot.'

He shook his head and carried on with his inspection of the plane, muttering about bloody Yanks and World War Two. 'What was that you said, Mac?' He stopped and turned. 'I said the bloody Yanks fought the war to the last drop of British blood and if I see him I'll tell him so.' I took his advice and went on board for a check. Good God! He wasn't kidding. Apart from the filth, which was everywhere, some of the seats were indeed broken, and I counted fifteen of them with either missing or torn seatbelts. A stewardess approached from the front of the plane when she saw me. 'Can I help you?' she asked, again with an American accent. She was blonde, thickening around the waist, and, not that I had any real objections, very obviously a little faded! 'Hi. I'm the Manager of the tour company. The names Vincent, and I'll be flying with you to

Palma.' 'Daphne,' she informed me. I mean, what else could she have been called?

'Where?'

'Palma. It's a Spanish island in the Mediterranean. That's where we're going.'

'Oh really? Nobody told me. Anyway, I'll be looking after you during the flight.' 'What, just you? Haven't you got a second to help you?' 'No. There is only me. But don't worry, ok? We'll be fine and anyway, we're only serving coffee. Bloody hell, I thought. This isn't just a cowboy-outfit; it's more like a circus. I dreaded to think what the passengers would say when they discovered the dilapidated conditions they would have to travel in. It was all right for me, it was my job, but those poor sods had actually paid for this. As it turned out, they were too weary to protest, although I could tell from their body language they were not too happy about it. I remember walking down the aisle trying to convince those passengers without seatbelts not to worry as they weren't really needed anyway. Imagine getting away with that one today! Captain Bilko must have satisfied Mac, the ground engineer, about the leaking oil, because we finally took to the air just after midnight. Admittedly the engines coughed and spluttered quite a lot and the passenger cabin sounded more like a creaky gate swinging in a gale force wind but we made it. There was a minor mishap during take off, one of the passengers' seats gave way and the poor woman fell backwards, together with the seat, into the lap of the man behind her. I helped her up while the aircraft was still at an attitude of thirty degrees - making it more than difficult - and gave her my seat, along with my apologies. We all of us then had to endure five hours of severe turbulence, and this in a clapped out, noisy old boneshaker of a plane that was only fit for the scrap yard. I thought at the time that had it been an animal you would have had it put down out of kindness. I noticed also, that even in the worst of the weather, the pilot didn't bother to light up the seat belt signs; either he knew many of them were broken and elected to ignore it or he was completely unfamiliar with standard safety procedures. My money was on the latter. The weather didn't ease until we were overflying Barcelona but at least, for the next forty- five minutes, we had a comfortable ride. I sat in the jump seat on the flight deck for the landing holding my hands over my ears because of the intense noise. Neither the pilot nor his co-pilot ventured to speak to me until the wheels had actually touched the runway and he was braking hard. It was as we were taxing he said to me, without even turning round, 'You got the cash to pay me?' I confirmed that I had it with me, resisting the temptation to ask him what he would have done had I said no; I had left it in Manchester? It was a tired bunch of passengers who gladly disembarked at Palma. I followed behind them, accompanied by Daphne, having paid Captain 'Bilko' his money. I reckoned it would probably take about half an hour to refuel the aircraft for the return flight to Manchester so I was able to have a word with the reps.

CHAPTER ELEVEN

STRANDED

An hour or so later I was sitting with our stewardess still waiting for the departure call, when the Captain called for Daphne over the Tannoy. I joined her on board, and a few minutes later we were airborne once more. About forty-five minutes into the flight Daphne returned from the flight deck, having taken coffee to the crew, to inform me, worry written all over her face, that the Captain wanted a word. By now experience told me that when that kind of a call came it invariably meant trouble.

'I didn't realise you were on board,' he greeted me with a grunt.

'That was the arrangement,' I reminded him. 'I fly back to Manchester with you and on arrival the tour boss will pay you for this sector. That is what we contracted for, if you remember?'

'Sure. I do now. Only now I got a better deal and we're not going to Manchester.' I couldn't believe what I was hearing so I asked him to explain. 'Well, it's kinda simple really. I got a telex in Palma telling me that the engine I dropped off at Toronto yesterday now has to be returned urgently to Buenos Aires, in Argentina.

So that's where we're headed. Toronto, and then on to Buenos Aires. So you're in for a long haul.'

'What about our contract? You can't just break it arbitrarily like that. We have passengers waiting in Manchester for this aircraft to take them to Malaga. What about them? Are you going to abandon them without a word?'

'I guess so. If you put it like that. But if you like I can try and get Spanish Air Traffic Control to send a telex to Manchester informing them of the change. That'll give your boss time to sort out his arrangements.'

'That's very considerate of you,' I said sarcastically. 'Obviously contractual commitments have no legal standing with you, have they?'

'Not when it comes to dollars, no.'

'And how about moral standards. It's okay is it to renounce binding agreements when it suits you, as a matter of convenience? And while we're at it, do you really believe it's either legal or justifiable to drag me along with you all the way to Canada with no notice?'

'Yeah, well, as I said, I didn't realise you were on board. I thought we'd left you back in Spain. So you can't exactly blame me for accidents, can you?'

'I bloody well can! You knew I was due to return with you to Manchester so at best, it's negligence. And what do I do when we arrive in Toronto? I have no money, I've given it all to you. How am I expected to get back to England?'

'Jesus! Are all you limeys like this? Always complaining? Look, fella, the tanks are full of gas, we're got a fourteen hour flight ahead us, and I sure as hell ain't making a stop just so you can jump off. So why don't you relax and enjoy the ride? We'll think of a way to get you home when we land in Toronto. And for Chrissake, give me a break will you and stop moaning.' I was in shock, feeling like one of those poor sods who was press-ganged into joining the Navy in the 17th and 18" centuries. I seriously wondered, in my naivety, whether or not I could sue him for kidnapping. What I did know for certain was that at the moment I was literally stuck on this aircraft, on my way to Canada, and there wasn't a bloody thing I could do about it. So I sat there fuming in frustration, even refusing Daphne's offer of a coffee. In fairness to her, she knew nothing about the change of plans; apparently she normally worked on the ground staff at Toronto Airport and had agreed to join this nutter of a pilot only at the last minute, and then only because of the money. Evidently, Mac had been right when he said this was a cargo company; it simply was not fitted out to carry passengers. But as I told her, at least she was on her way home; I was travelling three thousand miles in the opposite direction!

Then, miracle of miracles, a couple of hours or so into the flight his number four engine started spluttering. It coughed a few times, tried its best to remain operational, and then suddenly died a death by cutting out altogether. Our Captain Bilko was now up the proverbial creek without a paddle! He would have to make a tech. stop, either in Europe or North Africa. When he suddenly banked to port on his three engines I realised it was going to be North Africa. I made my way up front to ask him. 'Where are we?' I asked him. 'Off the coast of North Africa. We were just about to leave landfall when this bitch cut out on me. So we're making a touchdown at Casablanca. I'm notifying Traffic Control at the moment for landing permission. It's your lucky day, fella, you can get off there.'

'Why aren't we going in to Gibraltar, or even Tangier? Aren't they nearer?'

'They would be if they had the technical facilities to make repairs to this son of a bitch, but they're not equipped. So it has to be Casablanca. And anyway, I owe Gibraltar a whole pile of dough.' I wasn't convinced, if anything Gibraltar would have better facilities, seeing as they handled a lot of the BOAC traffic to the Far East. But I could hardly argue with him under the circumstances especially when he owed them money. It was more likely that he owed most airports money from previous transgressions.

We landed safely at Casablanca at seven in the morning and although what I had told him was true, I really didn't have any money, at least there we did have an agent for our North Africa ground arrangements, and I was sure they would help me to get home. But I had overlooked the fact that it was a Sunday and they were closed until the following morning. I pleaded with Bilko to lend me some money, but he coldly informed me that I wasn't his responsibility. Also you have to remember it was an era where credit cards were non-existent. Daphne very kindly gave me twenty Canadian dollars, about seven pounds, which was all the money she had on her. At least I would be able to get something to eat. The airport was virtually deserted at that hour, apart from a small crew of ground staff. So he wasn't going to get his repairs completed for quite some time, I was pleased to learn. And hopefully they would relieve him of whatever he had left of the cash I had given him in Palma. I hung around until nine am when the Air Morocco offices opened for an early morning domestic flight to Tangier and made contact with the Operations Manager. I didn't know him but when I gave him my business card and explained the situation he laughed at first, but then was very sympathetic and gave me a free ride on the scheduled flight. He also offered to send off a telex immediately to Manchester Airport and let Norman know where I was and what had happened.

So I found myself at Tangier Airport round about ten thirty local time still with my twenty dollars intact. I treated myself to a cup of coffee and a croissant, so relieved to be off that bloody Yank's plane and partly on my way home; it never crossed my mind that I had missed yet another night's sleep. From the airport I caught the bus into the centre of town; from there I walked it to the docks to check on the ferry times either across to Gibraltar or further up the coast to Algeciras, in Spain. A Gibraltar ferry was due to leave at one pm, so I tried my business card trick again. That was something else I learned on that trip, that generally speaking, people working in the travel industry willingly leapt to the rescue of fellow workers in trouble, regardless of its nature. Another free ride, a taxi to the Spanish border, followed by a further free ride on the bus to Malaga was no doubt helped by my ability to converse partly in Spanish with the coach manager. It was by now almost ten o'clock at night and I knew that there was no way I could make it home that night. I still considered, however, that I would be better off at the airport especially as my funds would not run to a night in a hotel. So I hitch hiked it part of the way and then walked the last couple of miles, arriving at a totally deserted airport by midnight. Fortunately, I had eaten at a cafe in Malaga, which was just as well because everything at the airport was closed. The cleaning staff woke me at five in the morning; one of them gave me a black, thick coffee from some kind of flask. It tasted quite horrible, but I was grateful. By seven the cafeteria was opening and I had enough funds left for breakfast.

A couple of flights were listed on the departure board but I got the impression they were out of date - one of them for instance, had an old Overseas Aviation departure still posted as 'delayed'. I managed a rinse in the airport's toilet but it was now two days since I had shaved, and I naturally had a 'blue chin' in those days. So I looked a bloody mess. Just after nine I wandered into the office of Iberia Handling Agents, yet again brandishing my, by now, magical business card. I explained my situation to the manager and he confirmed that if I drafted a telex to Manchester he would get it off straight away. Two hours later I had a reply from Norman to the effect he had arranged a seat for me on a Euravia flight to Gatwick, leaving Malaga at two o'clock that afternoon. Euravia was a charter company owned by "Captain Langton" and operated from Gatwick. He was quite a character, was Ted, and he owed his title to a trip he once took down the Thames.

The ticket, (showing me as a staff member of the airline) together with ten thousand pesetas about fifty pounds would be waiting for me at the Euravia check in desk at around lunchtime that day. Norman also confirmed I should be able to catch the overnight train to Blackpool, which I thought was damned considerate of him! He also informed me on the telex that our Malaga flight had had to be cancelled - due to no available aircraft; the returning passengers would have to be offloaded on different aircraft. Obviously, they had all left by the time I arrived at the airport.

It was a long wait but finally I was able to have a decent meal and the flight was a mere two hours late in taking off. We landed at Gatwick Airport at nine in the evening, in time for me to connect with the midnight train to Preston and then the milk train again to Blackpool. Finally, I made it home on the Tuesday morning, almost three days late, and four days without seeing my family or my bed. But, despite the stresses and strains, I had to admit it was quite an adventure.

By Friday of that week 1 was back in Spain again contracting for the following year.

Finally, the season came to an end. We were all exhausted and frustrated with the dilemmas besetting us throughout the summer months. Right at that moment we simply couldn't find an answer to the problems of flight. That is when Caledonian Airways came on the scene, which I will refer to later.

: Calle Navas, 52 — Telf. 216251   **ALICANTE**

UN CENTENAR DE AGENTES DE VIAJES INGLESES, EN ALICANTE

- ◆ Traen un objetivo: aumentar el turismo de invierno en la Costa Blanca

- ◆ Una compañía inglesa hará un obsequio a los novios que se casen en los meses de abril y mayo

- ◆ Las medidas económicas restrictivas impuestas a los ingleses no han afectado al turismo

- ◆ «El turismo de invierno tiene más poder adquisitivo que el de verano»

Vincent Cobb

GAS NEWS

Issue No. 15

The Thomson Hotel Santa Lucia in Palma Nova, Majorca

CLIENT PROFILE
THOMSON TRAVEL LTD.

Thomson Holidays is Britain's largest package holiday company and one of four integrated operations which form Thomson Travel Ltd., the travel and holiday division of The Thomson Organisation Ltd. The Organisation includes newspaper publishing, magazines, television, radio, oil and many other worldwide interests in addition to the travel division which operates its own airline, its own tour operating company, its own hotel chain and its own travel retailing company.

Thomson Holidays was formed in 1965 through the amalgamation of the tour operating interests of Skytours, Riviera Holidays, Gaytours and Luxitours. In 1972 Sunair and Lunn Poly were acquired and the latter now operates 42 retail travel outlets under the Lunn Poly name. Through this organisation, Lunn Poly also provides a business travel service which looks after international travel arrangements for some of the largest companies in the United Kingdom.

In 1976, around 800,000 British holidaymakers will travel abroad on holidays planned and operated by Thomson Holidays. Their destinations will range from the sunshine resorts of the Mediterranean and the Adriatic to North Africa, Egypt, the Greek Islands, the Caribbean, the Canaries and Madeira north to Moscow, Leningrad and Helsinki and eastwards to Siberia. At the same time, chartered cruise liners will travel south to Dakar and north to the Arctic Circle.

In order to establish and maintain high standards of quality, quality control, value for money and operating efficiency, the company set up a second holiday division Thomson Holidays (Overseas) to control the group's interests and activities abroad, and to operate its twelve hotels situated in the Balearics, Sicily and Malta. This company is responsible for all overseas contracts for accommodation with over 200 hotels featured in the Winter and Summer brochures, and for providing the services which cover such important elements as representatives, child minders, excursions and transfers. Thomson Holidays (Overseas) employs a permanent overseas staff of fifteen hundred.

Thomson passengers fly to their destinations from a wide choice of 11 U.K. provincial airports, mainly using the Boeing 737 jets from the company's own airline, Britannia Airways. Britannia Airways will fly more than 1½ million people, including passengers from other tour operating and overseas companies who rely on Britannia's record for efficiency and good time keeping for their own air charter arrangements. The airline is based at Luton Airport, Bedfordshire, from where it operates a fleet of 14 jets, providing a service for other companies in its own group and a charter facility for other non-affiliated tour operating companies. Britannia Airways also provides a maintenance service for other airlines based at Luton.

Once the overseas part of the holiday has been organised, the final holiday programme is constructed in co-operation with Britannia Airways. At this stage Thomson Holidays (U.K.), the group's marketing division takes over the important role of promoting and selling through the travel agents.

Until the oil and subsequent economic crisis, tour operating was one of the fastest developing industries in the world and the contribution to its expansion and development by Thomson Holidays has been extensive and far reaching.

They were, for example, the first company to introduce off-season weekend breaks in resorts normally only considered for summer holidays when they announced Winter Weekends in Majorca for £18. Prices for these weekends have been contained below inflation and represent equal if not better value today than they did six years ago. In 1972, Thomson offered the first charter inclusive holidays from the U.K. to Jamaica and in the same year began their incredibly popular Winter Weekends in Moscow from £29.

A year later they established yet another trend when they took a long exclusive lease on the Ulysses Line cruise ship, S.S. Ithaca, to provide inexpensive cruising to an eager market. Summertime holidays in established Lakes and Mountains Winter resorts followed soon after, along with a programme of long weekend breaks in European capitals. Thomson expanded into Winter Sports and is now a major U.K. Operator.

In 1974, the company introduced its Fair Trading Charter. This was a revolutionary move in terms of booking conditions which clearly set out customers' rights and contributed greatly to the security of holiday booking. In this, the company has lead the movement to help consumers and to work with the Government in formulating proper protection for the public — a move which other major companies in the travel industry have tried to echo.

In 1975, Thomson introduced three new holiday programmes: Fly Drive, Wanderer and A la Carte. And a second ship, the S.S. Calypso, former Southern Cross, joined the cruise fleet to make Thomson Holidays the second largest U.K. operator of cruising holidays.

In 1976, the Group introduced the most advanced systems technology to streamline sales, reservations and booking administration. Ten regional sales offices will communicate "on line" with a powerful computer via visual display units and land lines. It

Vincent Cobb

Brian Gurnett

139

A special reception for travel agents was held in the North British Hotel, Princes Street, Edinburgh. Organised by Sky Tours, about 200 agents and staff attended. Thomson Holidays Ltd. were represented by (from left) Mr Roger Corkhill, marketing director; Mr Vincent Cobb, manager; Mr Vincent Cobb, director; Zita Dwyer; Mr Brian Langford, promotions manager; and Mr Elis Evans, director.

Club 18-30 signs deal with public company

A DEAL was signed last week to take specialist tour operator Club 18-30 into the control of a public company.

A 65 per cent shareholding has been acquired by D. M. Lancaster, a publicly quoted company which is in the textile business. These shares were owned by chairman of Club 18-30, Mr. Maurice Harskin.

The remaining 35 per cent of shares are owned by Masters Investments, but D. M. Lancaster has an option to buy these which it is expected to take up shortly. These shares were sold by Mr. David Heard, earlier this year, who is now managing director of Hoss and has no connection with Club 18-30.

Managing director is Mr. Vincent Cobb, who joined the company in May having been with Thomson Overseas since 1965. He was one of the founders of Gaytours and Luxitours, which were taken over by Thomson.

Last week he was joined by another ex-Thomson man, Mr. David Harrold, who becomes marketing director.

Mr. Cobb explained that Club 18-30 wants to introduce new products such as skiing holidays, and buy some hotels. It now carries about 25,000 clients a year (mostly young, single people) and wants to expand to 50,000 within three years.

He said: "I believe the small to medium-sized operators are those in the middle of nowhere. Large operators don't need the backing of a public company, but if we're going to grow we need a big company behind us."

Mr. Cobb assured staff that the change in ownership "will in no way alter or influence the Club's management, its staff or its trading style".

● The summer 1980 brochure appeared this week, offering Miami as a new destination. Club 18-30 will move shortly to 133/135 Oxford Street, London W1.

Club 18-30 staff banished the Monday morning blues by offering copies of their newly-published summer 1980 brochure to shoppers in Oxford Street, London. Pictured, from the left, are: Ros Mack, Jeanne Billinge, Debbie Hume, Martina Andrews, Julia White, Ruth Davis, Mark Heard and Nick Johnstone.

Costa Blanca News

YEAR 1 – No. 47
Friday, October 25, 1974

REGIONAL WEE

THE MAYOR OF BENIDORM AS GUEST OF LORD THOMSON OF FLEET

"I have faith in the tourist industry. It doesn't matter we lose money for a year or two" says Lord Thomson

Thomson
Luxitours
EARLY AND LATE SEASON HOLIDAYS 1975

JET FLIGHTS FROM BLACKPOOL TO MAJORCA · IBIZA · BENIDORM · AND YUGOSLAVIA WITH INCLUSIVE COACH CONNECTION TO MANCHESTER AIRPORT

FROM AS LITTLE AS **£35**

Gaytours
Hotel Tested Holidays 1970

Pictured from left to right are: Vincent Cobb, Managing Director of Thomson Holidays Overseas, Señor Peter Devesa, Mayor of Benidorm, The Rt Hon Lord Thomson of Fleet. And Bryan Llewellyn, Managing Director and

New-look Club 18-30

CLUB 18-30 is heading for a year of consolidation, says Vincent Cobb, the man heading the London firm's new management team.

Cobb, well known in his former position as Thomson Holidays' overseas managing director, said that the company, which specialises in holidays for young people, will spend the next 12 months generally tightening up its operation.

The new Club 18-30 management, led by Cobb as managing director, also includes former Thomson men Jeremy Muller as finance director, and David Harrold as marketing director.

The Club is now backed by a publically-quoted organisation, D. M. Lancaster, following a sale of shares previously held by the firm's former boss, David Heard, to an Isle of Man investment company.

For the coming season, Club 18-30 is pegging its capacity at about 25,000 holidays to destinations in Greece and the Greek Islands, Spain and the Balearics, Italy and the United States.

Longer term plans, however, include the acquisition of a number of budget type hotels in areas to which Club 18-30 operates — this follows the purchase by the firm of the Hotel Castillo in Palma Nova — and a gradual expansion of the programme to include more regional departure airports.

CHAPTER TWELVE

Late 1962 Any Kite Will Do

The season ended with yet another tragedy. On the 7th October a DC3 belonging to what was then called Derby Aviation, crashed into a mountain near Perpignan. Thirty-one passengers, together with the crew, were killed instantly. All in all it was a shocking and disastrous summer for an industry reeling from a wave of bad publicity. One journalist described it as the 'summer of our discontent'. It didn't help matters when Pegasus Aviation, the small Luton based airline we regularly used for our short haul charters, went into liquidation in the November. I remember feeling quite sad about that; it was with that airline that I had flown over the Pyrenees in the unpressurised Viking, and it was with Pegasus that I had spent the night in Lyon sleeping on the floor.

I was also reminded of another 'little' incident with this airline when we were en route on one occasion to Barcelona. The flight was relatively on time, only about four hours down. A couple of the younger passengers had been drinking for quite some time and had become decidedly the worse for wear. Then they started playing up in the cabin and the stewardess didn't know how to handle it;

evidently one of them insisted he wanted to fly the plane so I went and had a word with the Captain. He was a really nice man, a bit on the large side, and he had these enormous hands that seemed to make the aircraft's steering column disappear when he gripped it. When I told him of the problem he suggested that I bring the passenger up to the flight deck and he would have a word with him. The inebriated client followed me, staggering up to the cockpit, where the Captain greeted him with a broad smile and asked him if he had ever flown a plane before.

'No,' he slurred, 'but I've always fancied it, and I don't think it's that difficult.'

'And you really want to have a go I believe?'

'I would, yeah. I think I'd be good at it.'

'Okay then.' And to my astonishment he climbed out of his seat and settled the piss artist in his place.

'Hey. What's going on? The bloody plane's not turning.'

'Oh. Sorry about that,' the Captain said. Then he leaned forward and manoeuvred a switch under the column, causing the plane to bank steeply to the left. 'There. I've turned off the autopilot. Now have a go.' 'Bloody hell,' I shouted. 'He'll kill us all!' By now the passenger was hanging on like grim death, desperately trying to control the aircraft and terrified when he realised he didn't know how to do it. 'Take it back,' he was screaming. Rather surprisingly he appeared to have suddenly sobered up. The First Officer just sat there shaking his head and laughing. 'I think he's had enough,' the pilot said, removing the client from his seat. 'You can take him back now, Vincent.' 'Jesus! You might have warned what you were planning to do,' I said. 'Oh. There was nothing to worry about,' he said casually. 'That little trick always works! I don't think you'll have any more trouble from him.'

Again, I will have to ask you to accept that this is a true story; it might appear wildly absurd, but the truth is that some of the pilots still believed they were fighting in World War Two.

In some ways he was right of course, except that this esteemed client threw up all over another passenger on the way back to his seat. I was only told later' and whether or not it was true I was never able to verify, that the First Officer had had control of the plane at all times and it was a device merely to cool the client's exuberance. One of the last flights the airline carried out just before going under, on which again I was a passenger, coincidentally, was on the Gatwick to Blackpool scheduled service when a Pegasus Viking mistakenly landed at Wharton Aerodrome, thinking it was Squires Gate Airport, Blackpool. Given that Wharton was a military installation wrapped in the 'Official Secrets Act', the Viking was quickly surrounded by Military Police and evidently was kept 'in custody' for more than twenty four hours while an investigation was carried out. We, the passengers, were given a lift home in RAF buses. Happy memories with Pegasus.

During the late October to December period we were experiencing great difficulties in contracting aircraft for the following summer season. There was a slim prospect at one stage of completing a deal with Caledonian Airways a new airline owned by Adam Thomson (now Sir Adam Thomson). They had started a series of flights in Sierra Leone and other parts of Africa using DC7Cs 'wet leased' from Sabena Airways, the Belgian national carrier. Wet leasing is an arrangement whereby the owning airline, in this case Sabena, lease not only the aircraft but also provide the crew and the engineering, thus making the new airline more of an administration operation. Although we were able eventually to contract with Caledonian for the 1963 season, unfortunately the timing was wrong for 1962. As a consequence we were virtually forced to deal with another new airline, called TASSA, an acronym for 'Trabajadores Aerolineas Sociedad Anonima,' or the Workers Airline. This Spanish airline, in addition to their mostly old equipment, had managed to acquire a couple of DC7s, which was the plane we had tried to negotiate with Caledonian. And what a bunch of cowboys they turned out to be! They almost made Overseas Aviation seem sophisticated and they gave Mac, the chief ground engineer at Manchester Airport apoplexy. Many of the pilots could not speak adequate English; time keeping was abysmal with aircraft constantly suffering technical problems as a result, once again, we had experiences of inadequate maintenance, and consequently involving us in disastrous delays. Also, rather like Overseas Aviation, they had no operational base to speak at Ringway so once again we were unable to communicate with anyone when problems did arise. I also got the impression at the time that the aircrew had a rather unique code when it came to the question of alcohol: no drinking within fifty feet of the aircraft!

We were offered 'Charlie "Whisky' by Captain Ted Langton (Every company had been offered Charlie Whisky!). This was an infamous old DC4 owned by Ted, which he used to 'lease' to his own subsidiary companies. The system was that he would charge excessive 'rent' to whatever airline Charlie Whisky happened to be operating for; then, when the airline got into financial difficulties, which was inevitable, he would bankrupt the airline, repossess Charlie Whisky and the cash flow and start all over again with a newly set up airline. Quite a clever arrangement really, except that people in the industry were starting to become wise to it and were refusing to have anything to do with the plane.

I remember one incident when Captain Gazubsky, Ted's regular pilot for Charlie Whisky, had to divert into Tunis airport through technical problems. The authorities, because of unpaid bills, immediately impounded the aircraft. A week later two unknown pilots arrived at Tunis airport and offered to buy Charlie Whisky from the authorities. All their credentials appeared to be in order, so the authorities agreed and a test flight was arranged for that day. Two representatives of the airport travelled on the test flight and to their horror they landed in Gibraltar, where Ted was waiting to reclaim his aircraft. They were helpless and consequently had to hand over the plane. The last anyone heard of Charlie Whisky was when Ted, through yet another of his airlines, secured a contract from the British Government to transport highly secret parts to the Woomera Rocket Range in Australia. Naturally the route had been carefully mapped out for Captain Gazubsky, avoiding any sensitive airspace. It was decided en route, either by Ted or Gazubsky, to shorten the sector length in the interests of profit and Charlie Whisky was 'escorted' down over Albania by a couple of MIG fighter jets!

So we started the season with some trepidation given the experiences of the previous year. A further sad development occurred in March of that year: A DC7C belonging to Caledonian Airways crashed on take off in Cameroon with over one hundred fatalities. The Industry seemed to be permanently involved in disasters of this nature. Personally, I felt sorry for Adam Thompson, the owner of Brit Cal.

Just prior to the beginning of the main charter flights I happened to be in Jersey sorting out problems in one of the hotels that the first of the groups was experiencing. It was a small but quite pleasant hotel owned and managed by an ex Squadron leader and his wife. Apparently he was turning out to be another nutter. Jersey seemed to attract them in those days. His wife told us that he was an alcoholic who, from time to time, went on a bender and found refuge in his own little world (I wish she'd said something before the season started!). For the previous two evenings he had turned up in the bar, drunk as a skunk, and proceeded to pull down the shutters of the bar, ordering everyone out. When his wife tried to stop him he punched her in the face. The clients, to say the least, were a bit indignant and were demanding that we find them alternative accommodation. So, with the wife's permission, I went along on the Friday evening at about nine o'clock accompanied by a local policeman and a member of the Hotelier's Association. Sure enough, the squadron leader staggered into the bar about half an hour later and headed for the shutters. Then all hell broke loose. The owner was grabbed, first by a couple of burly clients, and when he went to punch them the policeman arrested him - I never did find out what the particular offence was. The squadron leader then kicked the constable in the testicles and they tumbled to the floor. Good God, it was like

'Casey's Court'. Finally, the constable and the representative from the Hotelier's Association managed to drag the hotel owner out of the building and peace was eventually restored - that is if you overlooked the furious clients and the weeping wife. I recall the next day that the squadron leader's wife was asked to sign some medical form or other and the husband spent six weeks on a psychiatric ward of the St. Helier's hospital.

While I was on the island I took the opportunity of sorting out one or two other matters. I met up with Walter Collins, the owner of a rather palatial hotel called The L'Hermitage. Walter was a very nice man whom I became friendly with. Needless to say he gave us a few rooms in the annexe across the way from the main building. Some years later, Walter, offered me a job in Jersey. He and a number of other hotels had set up a company to handle the bookings of their hotels; I believe in all there were about ten of the major players. The job I was offered was to run the company, based in Jersey; Walter even offered me a very nice house that we could use. It was a very tempting offer. I liked Jersey very much but some unknown reason I turned it down. I still remained friends with Walter.

CHAPTER THIRTEEN

MY GUARDIAN ANGEL

After I had finished negotiating and dealing with odd matters with Patsy Sandford, our senior rep at the time, which took me until the Sunday lunchtime. We were also negotiating with Tantivy Motors for rental of one of their offices. In those days I was never able to pre- book a return flight since I was never sure of my arrangements. So, on the Sunday afternoon I turned up at Jersey Airport hoping I might scrounge a ride from Silver City, a small airline with a base at Squires Gate, Blackpool, who operated a scheduled service to and from Jersey. They had a departure scheduled for around three thirty that afternoon and it would have been a real piece of luck if they had a spare seat. Unfortunately they didn't. The flight was fully booked. That meant I had to thumb a lift from Channel Airways, the Southend based airline that still handled our Jersey traffic. The flight, scheduled for the same departure time as Silver City to Blackpool, was doing a kind of 'bus stop' service. First it was flying to Portsmouth, then to Bournemouth, and finally to Southend. I remember groaning with disappointment as I faced the prospect of yet another overnight journey to Blackpool. I managed to telephone

Norman at home to put him in the picture and ask him to let Pat, my wife, know that I was on the Channel Airways flight and that I would see her in the morning sometime. Both the Silver City and the Channel Airways flights were called simultaneously. I was standing, with my hand baggage, in the line for Channel Airways when I heard someone shouting my name. It was one of the Silver City check in girls, and she was waving a boarding pass.

'Vincent. It's your lucky day! One of the passengers has been taken suddenly ill so we have a seat for you.' She handed me the boarding pass. 'Here you go, have a good flight.' I almost kissed her with gratitude and literally stepped across from one line to the other with two boarding passes and joined the Silver City flight to Blackpool. I really couldn't believe my luck. Two and a half hours later we landed at Squires Gate Airport and I decided to treat myself to a taxi home, having saved the company all that money on train tickets. When I went through the front door I saw that Norman and Margaret, his wife, were in the lounge with Pat; her sister was also there with her. I remember they all had very sombre looks on their faces. I won't describe the emotional scenes that followed. Suffice to say that there had been a news flash that afternoon on television to the effect that the Channel Airways DC3 I was supposed to be on, had crashed on the Isle of Wight, killing the crew and nine passengers; the remaining five passengers being in intensive care badly injured who died later. If I hadn't believed in guardian angels before that experience, I did afterwards.

I had a number of near misses in various types of aircraft, with various airlines, in the years that followed, but never anything that ever put me as close to death as that particular Sunday afternoon.

I did in fact have a kind of mirror adventure early in the summer when once again I was on the scrounge for an aircraft seat. This time I was in Barcelona looking for a ride to Palma, with, of all companies, Tassa. The Iberia flight I had booked on was delayed indefinitely because of violent storms, when Operations informed me that there was a Tassa DC3 leaving any time now for Palma. This time my business card trick failed to work - the flight was not only fully booked but also overbooked. I tried persuasion, I tried cajoling, and I even tried a bit of bribery, all to no avail. There was no way I was going to get a ride on that plane. It was the next day before I heard that bad weather had forced it down into the sea between Barcelona and Palma with total loss of life. After the Jersey episode though, I don't think anything like that could ever have the same impact; I didn't really feel that I had miraculously avoided a disaster in the same way.

That summer was a nightmare of overbooking in the Spanish hotels and the inevitable flight delays, made considerably worse by the airline, Tassa, and their never ending catalogue of technical breakdowns. The real problem was that many of the Spanish hotels had over contracted their accommodation to tour operators without any regard whatsoever for the poor clients. We were particularly affected because by the time we arrived at the resort, often six or seven hours late, another competitor using a more reliable aircraft, say from Gatwick, would have beaten us to it and their clients would be occupying the rooms.

Benidorm and Mallorca were again some of the worst offenders; Lloret in the Costa Brava wasn't very different. It was true that a programme of hotel construction was under way across the whole of Spain, but that was a long way from fruition. In the meantime it was first come first served. We had one incident where the only place left in which we could accommodate clients was a boarding school in Benidorm that happened to be closed for the summer. The accommodation was in single rooms only, so you can imagine the reaction when clients saw where they would have to sleep. Also, they had to queue for all meals, as if it was a school canteen. The only thing they were spared was playtime and a bottle of milk! Oh, and did I mention that it was almost three miles from the Benidorm beach? We had to pay for coaches to take people to and from the beach, something we could hardly afford. Clients from every tour operator were literally spread all over the area; some were transferred to the nearby resort of Calpe, quite a pleasant little place but certainly not Benidorm. It was also about five miles away. Others were found accommodation in places like Playa San Juan, a beach with a couple of hotels on it, and hardly anything else, not far from Alicante. In Lloret de Mar, where one particular hotelier had oversold his hotel by four hundred per cent! This, I believe is how nearby resorts, such as Blanes and Calella were popularised, largely because the over bookings in Lloret prompted us to look elsewhere.

In Mallorca my friend Miguel Fluxa teamed up with Gabriel Escarrer to rent hotels; some of these were actually in stables and one hotel we used of theirs all of the meals had to be delivered as there was no kitchen. Kind of like 'Meals- on - Wheels' we had grown accustomed to in the UK for older clients. For the record, Miguel and Gabriel split up later; Miguel continued to own a few hotels but Gabriel – who started Sun Hotels throughout the world – sold his empire some years later and became a billionaire.

As an aside, it was Gabriel who rescued us when we were trying to complete a block of apartments in Cala Vinas. Without his help the building would never have been finished and a friend of mine and myself would be in dire straits.

However, the over-bookings went on for all of the summer. Week in and week out it was a constant battle to accommodate clients. We managed to find one hotel in Majorca where we paid in advance for the remainder of the season for the whole of the hotel, then appointed a permanent 'minder' to ensure that no clients other than ours were allowed access. What is it they say? 'Desperate men do desperate things.' It was pragmatism but the main thing was it worked, and it also gave us an idea of how to contract hotels for the following season.

But the summer couldn't possibly end without another drama in the air, and sure enough, it happened. I was returning on Tassa our favourite airline from Valencia one weekend with one of our managers; to spare his embarrassment I will avoid using his real name. Apparently he was quite a student of airports and their technical facilities including lengths and bearing strengths of runways. Inevitably the flight was delayed by the normal five or six hours, turning what should have been a night flight into a day flight. After some four hours we began our descent to Manchester Airport and a little later the fasten seat belt signs came on followed by the sound of the undercarriage coming down. Joe, I will call him, turned and said to me: 'That isn't Ringway down there.' I leaned across him from my aisle seat and saw he was right, although I couldn't recognise the airport. 'Yeah. You're right,' I agreed. '"Where do you think it is?' He had begun shaking. 'It's fucking Birmingham. He's trying to land at fucking Birmingham Airport.'

I ignored his blasphemy and said, 'I shouldn't worry. It's probably something and nothing. And anyway we can coach people to Manchester if we have to.'

'You don't understand,' he said, his voice trembling. 'This is a DC7C it can't land at Birmingham. The runway's too short. He won't be able to stop. Good God! You've got to stop him. He'll kill us all.' How many times had I heard that expression over the past years?

'Are you sure, Joe?'

'Course I'm bloody sure. I study airports, don't I? Tell the stewardess before it's too late.' Another thing I didn't mention was that the cabin staff didn't speak any English whatsoever. So I caught one of the girl's attention and in my somewhat broken Spanish said to her: 'Senorita por favor. Se peude decir al capitan que hay una falta. El Acropuerto abajo no es la ciudad de Manchester; es Birmingham!' (Could you please tell the captain that there has been an error, the airport down there is not Manchester it is Birmingham.) as the translation!

'Si, senor. Cuando tengo un momento, pero tenemos muchas activos en este momento.' She said she would as soon as she had a minute but at the moment she was too busy!

'Sorry, Joe, she says she's too busy at present. Don't worry.' I said reassuringly. 'We'll be all right.' It was too late by now anyway. We were on the threshold of the runway about to touch down.

Joe burst into tears and grabbed my hand for safety; I had to push him off. The pilot began to apply the brakes, and it certainly slowed us down, but obviously not enough. We just seemed to go on and on and on until finally we ran out of runway and went crashing through a hedge and into a field. There was a kind of stunned silence. I was getting out of my seat to cheek if everyone was okay when I noticed he had passed out. I couldn't believe it but he had actually fainted! There was pandemonium after that, with passengers trying to disembark. I had to almost force the stewardesses to lower the safety chutes and I then got on the intercom and made an announcement to try and calm everyone down. To some extent it worked, although there was no question of Joe panicking - he was still flat out! Fortunately, there were only minor injuries. Privately I could see the funny side of it, in the context of Joe's reaction; and shortly after that he left the travel industry and to my knowledge he never flew again. It can have that effect on some people!

CHAPTER FOURTEEN

1962 WINTER AND A 'SLEIGHT OF HAND'

The end of that season saw us with a busier than ever programme of autumn holidays, both for the Blackpool landladies and also the Jersey Hoteliers. For the first time we had arranged direct flights from Jersey to Mallorca. The aircraft we had contracted at that time, from Squires Gate and from Jersey, were prop- jet Viscounts from British United Airways - a luxury plane for us in those days. It was quite an innovation for the North of England to feature a plane of this quality. However, the last two flights fell somewhat short of the payload we had hoped for; in other words, we didn't really have sufficient passengers to justify an expensive aircraft like the Viscount. So Norman had this brilliant idea. There happened to be a Viking aircraft available that, if we contracted, for the return flight, could lower our return costs by half, thus turning a mediocre end of season into a profitable one. In Norman's view the change of aircraft was merely a minor inconvenience; he went as far as suggesting that 'these people' probably wouldn't notice the difference! The main concern at the time seemed to focus on having to return the

158

passengers to Blackpool a day earlier than planned, so he got around that one by offering clients a five per cent reduction on future holidays. I regretted not arguing with him, but I couldn't help wondering what world he was living in? Many of the Blackpool clients that autumn were staying in a very nice hotel in Terreno called the Araxa; in those days it would have been classed as almost luxury because it actually possessed bedrooms with private bathrooms, something that, as Norman remarked, the Blackpool landladies didn't even realise existed. Anyway, because there were so many clients staying there, Norman had yet another brainwave, or as I described it at the time, a brainstorm. He recommended that we speak to them all together about the flight and departure changes at the Araxa Hotel. I commented that I wasn't really concerned where we spoke to them as it would be Norman and not me doing the speaking. There was a near riot! Never had so little regard been paid to the feelings of Blackpool landladies. Norman had completely misjudged their reaction. After making his announcement in his friendly and relaxed style, he was suddenly surrounded by a group of very angry women, one of them, in fact, shoved him hard on the shoulder and sent the poor fellow flying over a lounge chair. Unless you've confronted a bunch of furious, middle aged and elderly Blackpool landladies, you couldn't possibly have any idea just how frightening it can be. I really thought they were going to kill him. But, all credit to Norman, his resilience was unbreakable. He held out a hand for silence, and bugger me if he didn't get it! 'Listen to me, will you. I regret this development as much as any of you do, but unfortunately there isn't a thing I can do about it. The original aircraft is not available, apparently because of some problems in Africa, so we all have to live with it.'

'British United, isn't it?' one woman asked. 'The airline you want us to fly in, isn't British United? Is it?

' Norman nodded. 'But there is no point in blaming them, these things happen, and it's no one's fault.'

'They only bloody well happen at Gaytours,' a large aggressive male- type snapped. 'And how come it's always us that gets it?'

'It's November, for God's sake,' another one added, 'you shouldn't have problems with aircraft at this time of year. And why haven't they got another plane they can send?' A very good point, I had to concede.

'Because at this time of the year the airline carries out a lot of troop movements to and from Africa and if something goes wrong, like now, all of the aircraft are already committed and we're stuck with it.' Which you have to admit, wasn't a bad response, and it had them floored for a moment or two. 'Well I'm going to complain to the airline,' the aggressive one countered. 'And to the bloody papers. It's not right this, you can't bugger people about and get away with it.' 'She's right,' yet another one chimed in. 'and anyway, I don't believe you, Norman Corkhill. You always were a bit shifty. You'll do 'out to save a bit of brass.' It went on and on forever and I'm afraid Norman was just not winning. However, as he had already told them, they could complain to whomever they liked but it wasn't going to change anything; the situation was a fait accompli. They might not have known exactly what that meant but they got the message and it provoked even more fury. In the end, we had to walk away and, using Norman's words, 'Leave the buggers to it.'

Only that wasn't the end of it. A group of landladies took themselves off to the local English paper, 'The Majorcan Bulletin', and gave an interview, providing chapter and verse of Norman's misdemeanours. It made the headlines the next day, accusing Norman Corkhill and Gaytours of fraud and suggesting that he personally had no right to be in the travel business. This time it was Norman who was seething. 'I'm not bloody well having this,' was his reaction. So we went off to see our Palma lawyer armed with the headline in question. We were promptly informed that libel, in this, the Franco era, was a criminal offence in Spain even if it were true! It also carried a mandatory prison sentence of five years. I didn't go with Norman and the lawyer to see the newspaper's owner, who turned out to be a retired British Major who was an alcoholic, but I was put in the picture later. Apparently, when the Spanish lawyer informed the newspaper's owner that he was about to be arrested for criminal libel and was facing a long prison sentence, he promptly fainted. Or at least he claimed to have done so. Norman said he was simply pissed and when he recovered he used it as an excuse to knock back a tumbler full of neat gin! He then proceeded to plead with Norman not to have him arrested, promising he would do anything he asked to prevent it. The next day's edition carried a headline apology, even larger than the accusatorial one, personally asking for Norman's forgiveness for the unwarranted and inaccurate attack on him. It praised Norman in every conceivable way short of saying he was the best thing that had happened to the travel industry since sliced bread, and I believe, had the lawyer insisted, he would have printed that also. After that edition, another of the lawyer's conditions was that he closed down the newspaper, which he did immediately. And Norman being Norman, he arranged for copies of the paper carrying the apology to be placed under every bedroom door of the Gaytours clients. On the whole it was a very unpleasant episode, and although my boss was publicly vindicated, it was the view of many people he was lucky to get away with it. Nevertheless, the landladies did return home a day earlier than scheduled on a Channel

Airways Viking instead of the more advanced Viscount and I was ordered to travel with them in case of further trouble. It turned out to be a bloody awful flight, flying through blackout clouds and violent turbulence. Fortuitously, the majority of them were too sick to complain much, but they made up for it when they got home. We were served with a writ from a group of landladies claiming they were misled by Gaytours and personally naming Norman as the culprit. Evidently they had been in touch with British United for support but they were disappointed; Norman had already contacted the Managing Director – would you believe it was Freddy Laker of the soon to be Laker Airways. He confirmed he would support Norman's story about delays in Africa and the writ actually got nowhere; it was just a shot in the dark and surprisingly many of the clients travelled with us the following year.

I put it down to experience. Norman put it down to saving a hell of a lot of money, In other words, he got away with it.

That winter we had a monumentally heavy fall of snow coupled with a severe frost. It went on for almost two months almost into the spring. We had made arrangements with a friend of ours in London to share his Paris trips; we had produced a small brochure advertising the short holidays.

One day, our friend set off to Heathrow Airport, on the old road. There were no motorways in those days. He got hit with a blanket of snow and had to abandon his car. He never saw it again; when the snow ploughs were trying to clear the way they must have picked up the small car and quite likely dumped it in a field. Needless to say, the Paris trips didn't go well s it was another waste of expenditure.

Norman always came up with these bright ideas.

CHAPTER FIFTEEN

SPRING/SUMMER 1963.
NOTHING NEW UNDER THE SUN

That year was a time of intense competition, with new tour operators coming into the market for the first time. Aside from the established operators, Doug Ellis (now of Aston Villa Football Club) was introducing Sunflight into Manchester, along with Cathedral Tours from Liverpool; Skytours was expanding also into Manchester for its first summer, having increased its Euravia Airlines fleet of Constellations. We were very fortunate because we had by now contracted DC7c's from British Caledonian. At the beginning of the season we organised a free day trip for our Northern Travel, along with a couple of friends of Norman. As anticipated the plane was about an hour late in arriving at Ringway so one of these friends of Norman complained bitterly to me about the delay. I told him, in the vernacular, that he was having a free ride to Mallorca, champagne and lunch included, and not having paid a penny. I asked him would he like me to cancel his trip: I was not prepared to put up with that kind of behaviour especially in front of our travel agents.

For me that summer was highlighted by the incredible support we had from our travel agency friends; without them we really would have been in desperate straits. I would like to add my thank you to all of them for coming to our rescue in those difficult days.

The expansion of the industry wasn't simply restricted to Manchester, although for some peculiar reason licences were easier to obtain from that airport. Gatwick was growing substantially, while airports throughout the country were embarking on upgrading programmes. Newcastle and Glasgow were two cases in particular, where Ted Langton of Skytours was scheduling flights to Mediterranean resorts for the first time. Birmingham Airport, together with Derby and Yeadon's Leeds/Bradford were not too far behind in development – Birmingham, would shortly be able to accommodate the Tassa DC7c's. Runways were being extended and strengthened to take the larger aircraft and new terminal buildings were being constructed to improve passenger comfort: a long awaited relief for those of us operating out of Manchester.

In addition to the growth in our own charter programme, we had also augmented our overall capacity by the introduction of air/coach tours to the Costa Brava via Southend and Ostend Airports. At the time we employed a contracts manager to organise the en route requirements of meals and overnight accommodation in France. Before the start of the season I received a call from one Andre Despegal, the owner of a small

Belgian coach company that we were employing to operate the programme (he was especially cheap!). He urged me to recheck the hotel and restaurant contracts as, having made an enquiry of the hotel in Lyon, and discovering that in fact, the contract did not exist, he was having doubts about the validity of the remaining agreements our manager was supposed to have secured. Apparently, his enquiry produced a comment from the hotel owner in Lyon that, 'yes, your man did speak with us regarding hotel accommodation for the summer season, but we informed him that we were unable to help him as we did not have the availability on the particular nights he required.' In other words, we were now in a bloody mess, with the first departure fast approaching and no arrangements for the clients in place. So I met up with Andre in Brussels and we set off by car to retrace the route. It soon became obvious that our lazy contracts manager had nothing whatsoever signed, and from what more than one of the establishments en route told us, his main interest seemed to be enquiring as to where the nearest brothels could be found.

Effectively, we had to begin all over again. There was no real problem with restaurants, there was an abundance of them on the Route National, but it was a different matter altogether in Lyon when we tried to arrange hotel accommodation. We spent two nights in the city, literally door knocking until, finally, the best we were able to achieve was allocating the parties to three, sometimes four, separate hotels, depending on the dates. I promised that I would cheerfully strangle that so- called contracts manager on my return to Blackpool.

On the evening of the second day we were having a meal in one of the local bars/cafes when suddenly, the doors at each end of the room shot open and we found ourselves surrounded by armed French police, who thrust everyone in the bar out into the street and into waiting Black Maria's. Andre and I protested vigorously, I remember personally informing the senior policeman that 'Je suis anglais, monsieur', which I thought was rather clever of me but which produced nothing but a hard shove in my back. We spent the night sharing a cell with a bunch of suspected Algerian terrorists. When we were finally released the next day, it was with a shrug rather than an apology and the recommendation we keep out of places like that in the future!

On the way to Paris we coincidentally came across the first of the coach air passengers; the coach had broken down, the beginnings of innumerable such incidents to occur throughout the summer. We wasted four hours before we managed to get it on the road again. Andre had to send off a telegram to the hotels in Lyon warning them of the delay. We spent a further four days in Paris, again door knocking, and again having to divide the groups into separate hotels across the capital. It was just as well that Andre was familiar with Paris or we would have had a real disaster on our hands. My clearest memory of that trip, aside from the exhaustion, was having to spend four days in Paris walking in heavy rain and getting soaking wet. The outcome of it was that I developed a kidney infection and had to spend the night in an Ostend hospital. I was advised by the doctors to stay there for a few days but I really couldn't spare the time to be ill. So I discharged myself the next morning, spent the day with Andre Despegal re checking the revised arrangements and then caught the overnight ferry from Dunkirk, crossing the channel in a force ten gale. It did wonders for both my back and my temper, and I was looking forward to confronting our contracts manager in Blackpool and strangling him, but on arrival I was to discover he had already done a runner, never to be seen again.

That year we moved offices into much larger premises in Blackpool.

A further pre-season problem arose when we realised that a series of eleven and twelve night holidays were not selling as we had hoped - just as well in the event because they were scheduled for the Costa Brava and we would have added to our hotel- overbooking predicament. The difficulty we faced was that we had programmed midweek and weekend holidays on the Caledonian Airways DC7C, which was fine for the weekend but had far too much capacity for midweek. Had we been compelled to operate both series on the bigger plane we would have lost a substantial fortune. To add to the problem, Caledonian Airways had nothing smaller, aircraft wise, than the one hundred and four seat DC7C and the Spanish authorities banned the use of two different airlines to fly the same series. Which blew a hole in my idea of operating the DC7C at the weekend and linking it to a smaller Fokker Friendship belonging to Autair Aviation, a Luton based carrier, for the midweek series. A perfect solution in theory but according to the airlines, of no practical value and therefore out of the question. So myself and a number of representatives from both Caledonian and Autair flew off to Madrid and met up with the European Licensing specialist there who handled the Spanish applications for most of the UK airlines. He managed to arrange for us to have an interview with the Spanish Air Minister, an air force general, and later informed us that it was a minor miracle that he had even agreed to see us. So the four of us spent the night before on the booze and I woke with a monumental hangover. Anyway, we spent a couple of hours grovelling, to the Minister, appealing to his better nature, and promising him that this was a special case which would never happen again. It was largely Gerd Paukner, the air- licensing specialist, who won the day for us; the general also made that very clear to us when he granted us our dispensation, telling me in particular that he never wanted to see me again. I am glad to say he never did! So once again good fortune smiled upon us. We managed to transform what would have been the ultimate financial disaster for Gaytours into a profitable season.

CHAPTER SIXTEEN

SUMMER 1963'
ANNEXES' - WORLD WAR THREE

In the space of a few short years, the growth of the package tour industry was becoming explosive. But it brought with it serious consequential problems with facilities and infrastructures throughout the UK, in the form of aircraft shortages, and more disturbingly in the Mediterranean resorts, where hotel development, together with parallel essential services such as water, electricity and sewage, were finding it impossible to keep pace. And to add to the problems the German and Scandinavian markets were starting to become a force to be reckoned with in the industry, bringing the already overstretched facilities in the resorts to breaking point. That didn't stop either airlines or, more particularly, resort hotels from trying to meet the swelling demand. The short-term answer was more and more overbooking and more and more disturbing problems with water and sewage in the resorts. It was relatively easier for the airlines to cope with the pressures; they either increased the number of rotations in a twenty-four hour period by the introduction of back-to-back night flights, or sub chartered aircraft from the foreign airlines.

Not that the type of planes featured had at that time improved very much; we were still in the era of piston engine, World War Two flying coffins, with little prospect of change in sight.

And for the hotels it was altogether a different story. The logistics of constantly trying to squeeze gallons into pint pots brought the industry, that summer, to a crisis point. If I considered that 1962 was a difficult year for overbooking, the present situation was intolerable. It was a season of unbelievable stress, for the clients, the tour operators, and although it was self-induced, for the hoteliers themselves. I really don't think they believed that most of the contracts they had entered into would be fulfilled, except for that disreputable rogue in Lloret de Mar who knew exactly what he was doing. When it happened, the majority of them were as shocked as we all were. Throughout Spain, which was most in demand, annexes became something of a norm. Hotels began using private houses, rooms that had no facilities other than a bed, anywhere where people could be accommodated, including in one instance (in which we were involved), an old stable. But even these crisis arrangements left tour operators a long way from solving the problem. As the season progressed towards the peak months of July and August so the pressures seemed to grow almost exponentially. Water became a problem, with almost daily rationing for the use of showers and baths and even then the supplies were intermittent and totally unreliable.

I personally remember one particular experience when I was taking a shower in a hotel before leaving for the airport. I had gone through the motions of soaping myself bodily before removing it with a strong spray of water, when without any notice the water just cut out and I was left completely covered in soapsuds. I made my way to the airport looking like a living advert for Persil. In the event I was forced to travel home, mostly in that uncomfortable state, although I did manage to wash some of the soap away with the aircraft's facilities, (the water was also off at the Airport!). I mention the incident merely to underline the sorry state into which the country's essential services had declined due to the pressure of expansion.

Water problems, needless to say, were not merely confined to washing facilities; they were also manifest in the various hotels' sewage systems with backwashing and blocked toilets a common occurrence. Much the same could be said of the electrical installations throughout Spain, some of which bordered on the downright dangerous. It would have been 'God help the clients' had we had a hotel fire! That summer, the problem of overbooking had spread to virtually every hotel in every resort. One evening we arrived at Valencia Airport with some ninety passengers to be told there was no point in making the four hour journey to Benidorm as there were literally no vacant beds in the resort. We spread the clients around a half dozen hotels in the city, taking whatever happened to be available. It wasn't quite a repeat of the Paris embarrassment but it was not that different. All I kept thinking was, 'poor clients, they deserved better than this.' I shot off finally by car to Benidorm to find out just what the hell was going on but it was four in the morning when I arrived too late to do anything until later.

The information we had been given in Valencia was accurate; every single one of our contracted hotels was overbooked, as was every other hotel in the resort. It took me all of the morning before I was able to contact our Resort Manager in Valencia and instruct him to bring the clients on the coaches, not to Benidorm though, as there was no point, but to a small village some twelve kilometres away called Palop. It wasn't dissimilar to transferring clients destined for a holiday in Brighton to Hayward's Heath. A further problem was that they were just not equipped for tourists in what, after all, was a typical Spanish village; some of the citizens had never heard of tourists. So there was no catering, other than a makeshift breakfast and we had to bus all the clients into Benidorm and back for meals, the beach and entertainment.

The whole situation was made worse one night in Benidorm when the sewage system in one of the hotels experienced a 'blowback' and literally exploded causing raw sewage to run rampant through the building forcing a mass evacuation. It also had a knock on effect because it was quickly followed by a similar Incident in two other hotels. It was a disaster waiting to happen and although temporary arrangements were introduced to try and solve the problem, it was years before a permanent solution was installed - would you believe by my old friend from years earlier, the Mayor of Benidorm.

Majorca wasn't a whole lot different. It was not uncommon for clients of every company to be accommodated in old closed down hostels, without any hot water or kitchens, with catering provided by a 'meals on wheels' system. That particular summer one Tour Operator, placed their clients in one the Terreno hotels, which was a closed down dangerous hotel with no facilities whatsoever. This was an act of sheer desperation. The Tour Operator was duly reported and the Ministry of Health ordered them to remove their clients – numbering around eighty persons. The hotelier and the Tour Operator were fined a substantial sum of pesetas.

One of the main culprits, I recall, was a four star hotel, called the 'Bahia Palace' in Mallorca, situated on the then prestigious Pasco Maritimo. I discovered, by having to search for some of our clients one day, that the hotel had placed them in a tiny apartment over a butcher's shop, accommodation in which the owner and his family were living. All right for them, perhaps, but hardly suitable for clients who had paid to stay in a four star hotel.

A further development that sprang from the expanding European market was the growing antipathy between the Brits and the Germans. The amusing adverts we have all seen on television showing the Germans grabbing all the sun beds before the Brits could access them was only a light-hearted reflection of the kind of things that were taking place back in the sixties. Again, it was overbooking that was the initial cause of the problem. For example, hotels that had only thirty or forty beds, and which in reality had contracted for something in the region of one hundred and twenty beds, discovered at that time that they could get away with using annexe accommodation, so they squeezed people into any available room, regardless of the standard or the location. Consequently, when it came to mealtimes, in particular dinner, more than one hundred clients would turn up all at the same time wanting to be served in a dining room with facilities for only forty. It was the Germans who wised up to this before the Brits. They began an early queuing system by posting sentries' outside the dining room on a rota basis, so when the dining room opened for the evening meal all the tables and chairs were immediately commandeered by 'those bloody Germans'. Of course the outcome was both predictable and inevitable to everyone except the Spaniards, who, as it was said about them in those early days, 'disguised abysmal ignorance with insufferable arrogance!'

It didn't take long for the fights to break out in various hotels, despite warnings from us given on a number of occasions to the hoteliers. I happened to make a point of visiting one of those hotels, some way from the beach in Arenal, to witness at first hand exactly what was going on. It was more or less as I described it - a forty-bed unit establishment in Arenal, accommodating more than one hundred people. At seven thirty in the evening some half a dozen German men were blocking the doors to the dining room, which wasn't due to open until eight o' clock; in fact they were actually manhandling the British clients away from the doors. Suddenly the Brits reacted and a fight broke out between the two nationalities. It was bloody and quite vicious with fists flying, feet going in to bodies on the ground; a German produced a knife and went for the nearest aggressive English man; he was pushed to the ground by two other clients. They were in fact Germans!

It showed no sign of stopping until I persuaded the hotel owner to call the Guardia Civil, the Spanish equivalent of the SAS. I was convinced, had they not arrived when they did, that someone would certainly have suffered serious injuries; it was possible we could even have seen a fatality. Ambulances were called and it took three of them in all to remove the casualties while the Guardia proceeded to take statements from the staff. All in all it took some time to sort out the mess. When I learned that the injured who had been sent to the hospital were in fact mostly Germans, I managed to keep a straight face. At one stage the hotel owner pointed towards me, so I went over to find out what he was saying. 'He is asking why you didn't do something to stop it?' one of the Guardia asked me. 'He says they are your clients and it was your responsibility to control them.' In those early days I didn't know the Spanish for 'tell him to piss off, (just as well I imagine because they would have thrown away the key) but I did manage to inform the Police that what the owner had told him just wasn't true. Only a small number of the clients were from Gaytours, the rest were either overbooked clients from other companies who weren't even supposed to be there in the first place.

Multiply that incident approximately fifty times and it will give a fairly accurate picture of what was going on in Majorca that summer. Multiply that number, again fifty times, representing the whole of Spain, and it was only surprising we didn't see the beginning of World War Three! The only area where violence did not break out because of overbooking was the Costa

Brava, probably because it wasn't an area yet popularised by the German's, and possibly because the use of annexes was limited by the size of the various resorts. There simply wasn't enough of that type of accommodation available.

The hoteliers' answer to the problem of overbooking was to ignore it altogether: as far as they were concerned, especially that lousy sod in Lloret de Mar. It wasn't their problem and if alternative hotel accommodation wasn't available, then tough luck. And the poor clients who suffered the most were the coach/air groups travelling on Andre Despegal's dilapidated coaches. They constantly broke down en route causing the clients, on more than one occasion, to arrive at the pre-arranged restaurant only to discover that they were too late and that it was closed. This invariably meant no lunch. One coach had to be abandoned in France, another two in Spain, and for years afterwards, one after another of the casualties could be seen rotting at the side of the main road near the Spanish/French border. And to add to their constant discomfort, the poor long suffering clients would arrive in their resort only to be told there was no hotel accommodation either.

I visited the area a number of times that summer, tearing out what little hair I had left. I remember once threatening one of the worst hotelier culprits with the police if he didn't find us some rooms. He merely shrugged and suggested I would be wasting my time as all the police cells were full anyway with overbooked clients.

That was the time when a whole coach- load of clients had no alternative but to spend the night sleeping in the coach outside one of the hotels waiting for vacancies to appear.

One evening, a couple of nights after that, I was in Calella de la Costa, which was effectively not on the Costa Brava but the Costa Dorada; it was only thirty miles from Barcelona. It was a scruffy little resort, largely undeveloped, and the one factor which had always discouraged me from volume contracting there was that it had a busy railway line running right between the town's main road and the beach. But of course that was before O/Bs, or 'over bookings'. Now we would be grateful for any small mercies and I was in the resort, actually, would you believe, trying to persuade one of the hoteliers to let me have some beds, not just for the remainder of the present season but also for the following year. He wasn't terribly interested; demand had become so high he was not worried. I happened to be leaving the hotel, disappointed to say the least, when an enormous storm suddenly burst on us and I was forced to shelter in his doorway. The water, very quickly, was flooding down the main street to a depth of probably a couple of feet. That was when the owner's wife, who was heavily pregnant, appeared in the doorway, an anxious expression on her face. I asked her what the problem was and she informed me that she had left her two children alone in her apartment whilst she had slipped round to the hotel for some urgent provisions. Her husband, who I had just left, was stuck at the hotel and unable to help. So I offered her a piggyback! She shrieked with laughter as I fought against the current with water now up to my thighs. I couldn't really understand exactly why she was laughing. She was a very heavy woman and once or twice I stumbled and almost fell into the fast running water. All I could think was, 'the things I have to do to earn a living!' Eventually we made it back to her apartment and she offered me a pair of her husband's dry trousers, which I hastily declined. What she insisted on doing though was telephoning her husband at the hotel to let him know that she was safely home, describing how I had helped her. The result was that he asked me to return to the hotel where he promptly gave us an allocation of beds for that summer and a contract for the following year. I became good friends with the family after that; the woman had a little girl a couple of months later. Her daughter is now married with children of her own.

I then received an urgent call to go to Lloret de Mar, further up the coast. Our senior rep. there had let our agents know there was a serious crisis but after all the other things going wrong I was really pissed off when I learned that the serious crisis was a 'haunting'. Eileen, the rep. in question, insisted that the bedroom that we had rented for her was having 'visitations'; ghostly figures appeared at the end of her bed each night, and now she was refusing to remain in Lloret unless we did something about it. What the hell was I supposed to do with a case of the DTs? And how the hell could I get rid of the Pink Elephants that appeared nightly at the end of her bed? But I knew we couldn't manage the season without her. Then I had an idea; recruiting the services of a local priest - being the good Catholic boy I was! Understandably he refused, informing me that the Church did not carry out exorcisms in this day and age; he was still very reluctant even after I pressurised him, but when I explained that the 'spirits' were more a case of vodka than a case of haunting and that we would be giving him a substantial sum some money, he agreed to carry out a kind of alternative exorcism. Again I had a job keeping my face straight but then so did the priest. It ended with him blessing the room with Eileen on her knees her hands joined in supplication.

Regrettably, the results only lasted for two nights and then the demons were back at the end of the bed. The only solution after that was to replace Eileen. That was difficult to achieve but eventually I transferred one of the other reps from Blanes.

All in all it was an unparalleled season for quality control. I would have to go as far as to say there wasn't any. Thanks to the disreputable business practices of the Spanish hoteliers, clients were forced to suffer intolerable hardships. The more worrying feature was that there was no immediate sign that things would be any better the following year. All of the tour operating companies were particularly concerned that the problems - resulting in an unprecedented deluge of complaint letters, where starting to be coupled with claims for compensation, and almost daily exposure in the national press - and if this continued people would be discouraged from re booking for 1964. It was commonly accepted in the industry that things would have to change dramatically if growth was to be sustained. New hotels were needed urgently, infrastructures in the resorts desperately required updating, and finally, every one of us was aware that the standard of aircraft flying our passengers was becoming increasingly unacceptable. Already the national flag carriers had introduced the new generation of fan- jets to their fleets, even on the short haul routes across Europe. I stood alongside a Boeing 707 one evening at Madrid Airport and I was overawed by its sheer size. We had never seen anything like it.

But to bring about the much-needed changes to the industry we first needed to look more closely at ourselves. We were now producing glossy coloured Holiday Brochures, full of misleading pictures. For instance, it was common practice to fly a well - known model out to one of the resorts and photograph her, in the company of one of the good-looking locals, dining outdoors on a non-existent hotel balcony, on a feast of non-existent lobster and other exotic sea food dishes. Hotels were photographed from the most flattering of angles, Both outside and inside; as our advertising agents at the time tried to constantly impress on us: 'We were selling happiness and people just did not want to see reality in brochures.' It also has to be remembered there was no Trade Descriptions Act in those days, so distorted photographic presentations, together with exaggerated descriptive copy, were perfectly acceptable tools with which to sell our products. No one in the industry would have accepted for a second that we were deceiving the clients; this, after all, was the new form of marketing. Our adverts, which also had a great deal of spin put on them, again by the new breed of advertising agents, had begun appearing on Granada Television for the first time. There was an unspoken philosophy amongst the general public in the sixties; if it had appeared on television it just had to be good! So what were we to do? Inform the clients that they would mostly be travelling in old, dilapidated, World War Two aircraft? Let them know that the hotel photos and descriptions in the brochures were steeped in syrup? Like the swimming pool described as 'Olympic size' but in reality was suitable only for children - in fact it was far too small for the volume of adults in that particular hotel! Or should we be really honest and inform them that generally speaking the food in the vast majority of hotels, particularly in Spain, was virtually inedible and they stood a good chance of food poisoning? Or, how about overbooking? Perhaps they should be forewarned that there was a risk that they might finish up sleeping in hovels, or in tiny cramped rooms, miles away from the hotel of their choice? We, all of us, quickly came to the conclusion that holiday brochures could never fully impart the truth.

What our task had to be, as a matter of some priority, was (as far as was realistically possible) to match the product with the expectations we had created in people's minds. One of the first things we did to correct our image of being a misleading industry was to substantially reduce our bed allocations in resorts such as Benidorm, the Costa Brava, and selected areas of Majorca. We re -contracted only those hotels with which we had enjoyed both long and satisfactory relationships and in specific cases we placed deposits up front by way of guaranteeing occupancy. In addition, we adopted the innovation of 'leasing' apartment blocks, making separate catering arrangements in advance, which we knew from experience would be reliable. We also took the decision to increase our presence in areas where no evidence of overbooking had appeared; a good example of this was in Ibiza. We were helped to a large extent in Ibiza by Vicente, who became a close friend of mine. It was a great tragedy that Vicente, some years later, was involved in a car accident on his way back from San Antonio to Ibiza Town; he completely lost his eyesight and was blind for life.

That was the time we changed our hotel contracting policy by the recruitment of a specialised contracts manager; that winter we had taken on an experienced Spanish hotelier, Ramon Adell, a close friend of mine, who would be based in the North of England, and to whom we gave responsibility for the whole of the contracting policy overseas together with the recruitment and training of our reps. Ramon stayed with us for a number of years finally leaving us to manage two hotels in Cala d'en Bossa, very nice hotels close to Ibiza Airport. Of course we realised that it would be impossible to eliminate the overbooking syndrome completely, particularly as those hoteliers who were 'serial offenders' were still in business. On the contrary, should the market continue to expand as it had done, the situation was likely to worsen, especially since the hotel building programme in the resorts was, at least at the present, just a token gesture. But to our credit we had taken steps to reduce the problem dramatically; we could only hope the expansion plans in the hotel industry would be realised.

What we had to do eventually was to organise a group of tour operators, ourselves included, and arrange a meeting with the Minister of Tourism in Madrid. He was very sympathetic and offered to help. The fact that he did nothing was actually irrelevant because it did bring to the attention of the Government there was a serious problem throughout the resorts. In turn that in itself brought pressure to bear on the recalcitrant hoteliers who were persistent over-bookers.

We also re-examined our policy regarding aircraft and airlines. Quite a number of tour operators had suffered at the hands of Overseas Aviation and Tassa and although for different reasons they were by now long departed, as I have already commented, the substitute aircraft were still ageing and totally obsolescent. We had already transferred a substantial part of our programme on to the Caledonian Airways DC7C, a substantial improvement on the older Argonauts and DC4s but still in itself an old plane. We had also contracted with Luton's Autair for some of the shorter haul routes using the Fokker Friendship; a good aircraft but not suitable for the developing market we were envisaging. The consequence of this in depth re-evaluation was a decision to open discussions with British European Airways to explore the possibility of entering into charter agreements with the National Carrier. No company had ever succeeded in this direction before now.

The finale to the season came when I found myself, yet again, accidentally involved in another mishap in the air. I thought at the time it had been too good to be true. I should have realised by now that emergency landings were an occupational hazard. I was in Ibiza, trying to get a flight back to Palma. The Iberia flights were all full as usual so the only available option was to fly on Tassa, something I had vowed I would never do again. But, something about necessity overcoming resistance, forced me to accept their offer of a lift. It was a late evening flight, the weather was good and visibility was perfectly clear. It wasn't a long flight on the DC3, probably no more than forty-five minutes, and we began our descent more or less on time. I was tempting providence by beginning to believe it was my lucky night when suddenly we were in the sea about two hundred yards from the shore. There was no warning; it was as if we were making a perfectly normal landing. My thoughts at that moment were that a mistake had occurred and this hadn't really happened. But it was true all right. Evidently our intrepid pilot had mistaken the reflection from the lights on the Portixol Road as the threshold lights of Palma Airport. I mean it could have happened to anybody, couldn't it! But you will have to believe this is a true story. Strangely enough there was no panic amongst the passengers; it is as though in those situations, and I had by now experienced quite a number; the innate nature of shock gains its own stranglehold and paralyses the victims. Movement after that is more by reflex than intent. It took only a few moments and we were all in the inflatable life rafts other than one middle aged lady, who was arguing with the crew that she had forgotten her handbag and was insisting she had to go back into the cabin to retrieve it. Funnily enough, I had my briefcase clutched tightly under my arm. The plane was already beginning to sink as the captain screamed at her to get into the life raft. Regrettably she chose to ignore him, and sank, along with her bloody handbag, drowning in her own foolishness. It was very sad, made worse for everyone because it was completely avoidable. Other than that dreadful tragedy we made it safely to the shore; we were so close to Palma I could have caught a bus back to the hotel! After that experience I never did fly Tassa again, and in fact, a few months later they went into bankruptcy.

The only redeeming feature for me that summer was that Norman appointed me to the Board of Gaytours; I was also made Managing Director and Norman took up the position of Chairman. We also bought a local travel agent, called Luxitours. This was an IATA Agency that was in serious financial trouble and initially we used it merely as a travel agency. But later, we mounted a programme of Inclusive Tour Holidays for Luxitours, almost as a competitor with Gaytours.

Vincent Cobb

CHAPTER SEVENTEEN

1963/64 DISAGREEMENTS

That winter, Gaytours moved its Head Office from Blackpool to Manchester, and opened a large travel shop on Deansgate. I personally argued against it, partly on the grounds of cost, and partly because I didn't believe it was necessary from a marketing point of view. I lost the argument and Norman left me in the wilderness of Blackpool to launch the new product for Luxitours. At the time Norman and I we were hardly speaking to each other and I believe it was also because I questioned whether he wanted the move for some more personal reason. Was he up to his old tricks?

The new programme had limited success, sufficient to justify its launch, but hardly exciting. From memory I believe Luxitours had a capacity of around ten thousand seats for the 1964 season and we eventually sold two thirds of them. Sales in Manchester for Gaytours that winter were not going too well either. Of particular concern was a programme of eleven and twelve night holidays we were featuring with direct flights, for the first time, from Yeadon Airport, Leeds. It was at that time that Norman decided to introduce a crude type of computer system into Manchester. It was a kind of panel/board where you plugged in wires and effectively that became the memory. ICL Computers must have had a good salesman at the time because it was a bloody shambles; the records this machine was producing were completely unreliable and inaccurate. Some flights showed as full when they were only fifty or sixty per cent sold, others showed empty seats when it was clear they had no availability. Coupled with the poor sales from Leeds/Bradford, which had separate manual controls, also unreliable the mechanical monster corrupted the figures. The administration system was in very real danger of collapsing. As Norman had virtually ostracized me because of our disagreement I had very little to do in Blackpool. I refused to have anything to do with his stupid computer system, which if anything added to his irritation with me, and I began seriously to consider joining a competitive company from which I had received an offer. The travel industry, even in those days, was very much a gossip shop, and news of the row between Norman and myself was the talk of the North, especially amongst the many friends I had in the Travel Agencies. I felt he had worsened the situation when he recruited a replacement for me; someone who had absolutely no experience, and who, almost immediately, managed to achieve a complete breakdown in the system. By now it had begun to reflect upon the Luxitours image, with a deluge of complaints landing on my doorstep from travel agents, all concerning the inefficiency in Manchester's admin procedures. Finally I gave Norman a call - we hadn't spoken for three months - to tell him that I had had enough and that I was about to accept another, very good, job offer in Manchester. He then proceeded to swear at me, accusing me of being irresponsible for leaving the company and using his own words, "Leaving him in the shit!" In my inimitably arrogant style, I promptly told him to piss off, pointing out that he was the one who had effectively disenfranchised me and who had caused the breakdown in systems control. We resolved the row by agreeing to meet in the Manchester offices that same day.

Norman was in a hell of a state when I saw him; he really didn't know whether he was on his head or his arse. The replacement manager had been summarily dismissed, other staff members, some of whom had transferred across from Blackpool, were leaving in indecent haste and all in all it bore the signs of a disaster. The end result of our meeting was that we shook hands like a couple of naughty schoolboys. Norman gave me a substantial rise (something, by the way, that was long overdue, and which, as I only discovered later, that Pat, my wife, had attacked him over) and I was given my old job back but it meant having to commute to Manchester. I spent the next four weeks burning the midnight oil trying to make some sense of the shambles. The only thing I could do was to abandon the so-called computer and revert to a totally manual system. It literally meant starting from scratch and going through every single booking form by hand and recording the details on a flight seat plan I had drawn up. It was cumbersome and painfully hard work and I worked many times into the night. Eventually we managed to recover some semblance of efficiency, following which I had to go through what was known in the industry as 'flight consolidations'; or making a bad situation into a reasonable one. I cancelled all of the flights from Leeds/Bradford and absorbed the passengers on to the parallel Manchester series, thus giving us acceptable load factors. I offered the Yorkshire clients free coach arrangements to and from Leeds to Manchester and return, and to my relief the vast majority accepted the change. I also believe that the more modern aircraft, the BEA Vanguard, on the Manchester flight might have had something to do with it. Finally, I had to re-staff the Manchester office to replenish the depleted team and arrange a crash course in the manual systems so we could fully get back on track. I also began discussions with ICL Computers regarding the new generation of systems coming onto the market and, as a result, entered into serious negotiations to introduce the 1900 Punch Card system for the following year. It would have a storage capacity of I6K and would require an air-conditioned office space of around five hundred square feet. Today it is rather like comparing a postage stamp with the Post Office Tower. Next I cancelled my old friend Andre Despegal's operation of the coach travel end of the coach/air programme and switched the whole series to a Dutch Company that had a modern up to date fleet of comfortable coaches. I was sorry to have to say goodbye to Andre he had been a good friend in many ways. But times do change and poor Andre simply wasn't recognising that fact.

In February of '64 a Britannia Aircraft, belonging to Cunard British Eagle, crashed at Innsbruck Airport. All 75 passengers on board, together with the crew, were killed outright. As was the common reaction in the industry when accidents like that occurred, especially when they involved fatalities, there was a feeling of personal loss and grief, almost as if we had all lost a friend.

On the positive side, that summer we were given the licence on a Skytours series to Malaga. Ted Langton was unable to sell the series from Manchester so reluctantly he transferred the licence to Gaytours.

By then Captain Langton had thrown his Constellation aircraft on the scrapheap and bought a job lot of Britannia's on the cheap from BOAC, who had upgraded to the Boeing 707, the new long-haul fan jets. The Britannia, known in those days as the 'whispering giant', was a considerable improvement on its geriatric predecessors. Anyway, the point was that for some reason Skytours experienced difficulties in selling their portion of the flight while we, on the other hand, had a sellout. We had operated for some time now a two-centre holiday to Torremolinos and Tangier - a week in each resort. I remember an incident the previous year when the DC6 aircraft we had charted touched down in Malaga from Tangier for refuelling and loading of the passengers joining in Malaga, when it exploded! Apparently the man carrying out the refuelling had forgotten to earth the bowser - the tanker - when a spark of static electricity blew up first the tanker and then, almost immediately, the plane. The poor man was killed instantly of course, but the only other casualty was the luggage of the clients who had joined the aircraft in Tangier.

Where was I? Oh, yes. I was on one of the first Britannia flights to Malaga, and we had filled the whole aircraft with our clients. I happened to have Margaret Corkhill, Norman's Wife, with me, and part of the way through the flight she asked me if I had noticed anything odd about it. When I replied, no, she informed me that apart from the stewardesses she was the only woman on board! It was really from that point on that we started to become aware that our generic name was going to cause us problems. Later that summer our advertising agents showed us a periodical currently published in America called 'GAY NEWS', and apprised us that the name was in the process of adoption by the international homosexual community, which explained Margaret's puzzlement about being the only female on board that flight. It served to warn us that unless we particularly wished to 'specialise', the time would come when we would have to consider a change of name.

On the whole, things were going well for us that summer. Generally speaking, our aircraft operated more or less on schedule and the contract with BEA for the Vanguard aircraft had given us a huge boost in sales. We were the first company ever to operate charter aircraft with the National Carrier. As we predicted, this was the way the industry had to go if it was to sustain its growth. People were already becoming more experienced in foreign holidays, not on the massive scale we eventually witnessed during the nineties, but enough to make their requirements known. As I have commented, Skytours had already begun a substantial change of image by re equipping their aircraft fleet. Ted Langton was making similar moves on the hotel front by investing large sums of money in assisting developers in the building of new hotels - something the Spanish government never did. This new generation of hotels would be large, larger than anything seen before, to cater for the mass market. They would all have private bathrooms and balconies, swimming pools, and extensive lounge and bar facilities to allow for in house entertainment. What Ted Langton also adopted was the procedure of paying substantial deposits to hoteliers in exchange for guaranteed bed contracts, and a schedule of building improvements that the hotelier promised to undertake during the winter months. If I were asked to name the one person who had contributed the most to the development of the mass market for package tours I would have to say 'Captain' Ted Langton. He was the man who not only had the vision to anticipate growth but who also had the courage to help shape the industry's future by risking very considerable sums of his personal capital.

The problem for us, and other tour operators at that time, was that we could not compete; we simply did not have the resources at our disposal and some of us, to be frank, began to fear for our future survival. And as a result, most of the companies continued to suffer the problems of overbooking. Aside from Ted Langton's innovations the hotel industry in Spain was making little or no attempt in 1964 to keep pace with demand. And the bottlenecks inevitably continued, especially in those more culpable resorts such as Benidorm and the Costa Brava. Fortunately, as I have already mentioned, we had planned in advance to bypass much of it by reducing bed allocations and contracting for apartment blocks where clients, especially families, had the benefit of superior accommodation. Our main problem that summer was buying toilet rolls and soap and organising cleaning and linen facilities! Ramon, our contracts manager, spent virtually the whole summer in Benidorm overseeing these arrangements.

It was a particularly hard summer for me; either I was commuting about a hundred miles a day to and from Manchester or I was abroad, because Ramon was entrenched in Benidorm, struggling with hotel contracts for the following year and ongoing operational problems in resort. Those were the times of fifteen or sixteen hour days. In fact the one period of rest I clearly remember was enforced; I contracted a particularly bad case of food poisoning in Tossa de Mar, a Resort on the Costa Brava, and spent two days on a drip in the local hospital practising my Spanish, convinced it was one of the hoteliers seeking revenge! Food poisoning was, medically speaking, non-existent in Spain. Even on the odd occasion when half the guests in a hotel went down with a stomach illness, the local doctors, almost as if they had been pre rehearsed, diagnosed too much sun and booze. Gastroenteritis was equally a non-existent illness, caused by the same overindulgence. One particular incident with which I was concerned involved a number of children in a hotel who went down with severe stomach cramps and dehydration. More than a dozen of them had to be hospitalised, two or three being seriously ill. It wasn't until I arranged for a senior doctor from Barcelona to examine them, that staphylococci, a pretty vicious bacteria that has been known to kill children, was formally diagnosed. Luckily, all of the children recovered, but it was a very nasty experience for everyone. It turned out that the particular hotelier concerned had been buying unpasteurised Milk on the cheap from a local unlicensed farmer. The hotelier was fined heavily and I believe the farmer spent time in prison.

It served as a warning shot across the bows of a number of hoteliers who prior, to the publicity this case attracted, seemed to think that Louis Pasteur was a French Painter and that bacterium was found only on soiled linen in hospitals.

CHAPTER EIGHTEEN

'NEVER ON A SUNDAY'

There was another maxim in Spain about medical conditions: Never die on a Sunday! I happened to be in the Calamayor Hotel in Majorca one Sunday afternoon trying to contact Pablo, the manager. The receptionist was busy on the phone trying to find him, while our local agent and I waited at the desk. Opposite was a family seated in the small lounge area, having a coffee and a cognac. I watched one of the men raise his brandy glass to his lips, take a sip, and then die. I whispered to Antonio, the agent, 'That man has just died.'

'What? What man?'

'That one. Look. The one sitting opposite us.'

'Good God! You're right.' He then turned and whispered the news to the consejeria, who promptly shouted, in a panic: 'Dead? Who is dead?'

Of course the family couldn't help but hear him, and I cringed as I watched one of the women gently nudge the dead man when he failed to respond to her question. Naturally he fell forward, banging his face on the coffee table, and smashing the brandy glass. 'Henry,' the woman said in a shocked voice. 'Are you all right, Henry?' I'd heard some bloody daft questions in my time but that one took the biscuit. It was perfectly obvious Henry was far from all right; the poor bugger was clearly dead.

We stayed at the reception desk and watched the drama unfold. The widow fell to her knees and tried her best to shake Henry back to life, all the time continually asking him if he was all right.

'Madam,' the consejeria helpfully pointed out to her, 'I believe your husband is dead.' Then the hysteria began. Two other ladies in the group joined in the tears. One of the men demanded that the hotel call a doctor immediately and Antonio was trying to ask the consejeria whether he had found out where Pablo, the Manager, was?

'He's fishing,' he told him, irritation in his voice. 'He will return later in the afternoon.'

'Well I have to leave,' Antonio told me. 'Are you waiting here?' I said I would because I particularly wanted to speak with Pablo. I arranged to meet up with Antonio later. In the meantime the drama was still going on, but the consejeria was able to tell the group that at least that an ambulance was on the way, though Christ only knew what he was expecting them to achieve.

I went for a coffee and was sitting at the bar some time later when I heard the commotion coming from the reception area. So I wandered out for a good old fashioned nosy in time to hear the consejeria informing the widow, in his broken English, that the ambulance men, who were standing there somewhat impassively, had said that as her husband was definitely deceased, as certified by the medics, there was nothing they could do.

'What do you mean?' she demanded tearfully. 'They have to take him to hospital.'

'No, madam, is not possible as today is Sunday.' I think she already knew that and it certainly meant nothing to me until he explained in Spanish that the morgue is always closed on a Sunday and therefore dead bodies could not be moved. There was simply nowhere to take them. When I explained this to the widow she naturally wanted to know what they were going to do with her dead husband? Could they perhaps find another room for him? The consejeria shrugged his shoulders and informed her, somewhat dismissively I thought, that no, that was not possible as the hotel was fully booked. 'But where can he stay?' It seemed to me to be a reasonable question under the circumstances, but evidently the receptionist thought differently. 'Same place as last night, Madam. In bed with you!' Bloody hell! I thought the roof would fall in. 'What?' she screamed. 'You can't do that. He's dead. You can't put him in bed with me.' I translated for her, which prompted another shrug from the consejeria. 'It's up to her,' he stated. 'Either he goes into her bed or he stays here for the night.' As diplomatically as I was able - I must admit it was difficult not to see the funny side of it all - I informed her of the options. Eventually she agreed that he could not stay where he was, so she asked for some assistance in getting the body upstairs. The two ambulance men had already left, so two of the men in the party had to help out. Now, one of the problems with the Calamayor Hotel was that it was very old, and the lift they had was one of those old -fashioned gate lifts that held only three people at a time. So it was a hell of a job for the men to squeeze themselves and a body into such a small space; in fact it proved impossible, so the only alternative was to carry him up the narrow, winding staircase. (I feel I should mention here, before I am accused of Plagiarism that in 1964 Fawlty Towers had not been created! And that this indeed is a true story.). It took an age to negotiate those narrow stairs; they had three flights to climb but finally they managed it and successfully installed the dead man in the wife's bed. I followed the group up the stairs in case any disasters occurred and I might be able to help. To make matters worse, they had been sharing a double bed, so the poor woman was going to have to sleep next to him. When the widow asked if we thought that the deceased should be undressed we assured her that it wasn't really necessary. To be perfectly honest, the arrangement was not something I personally fancied. Finally, it was all over, and we retreated to the bar. A little later Pablo arrived from his fishing and joined me for a coffee, when his consejeria explained the events to him. He didn't find it at all funny, but proceeded to swear at the receptionist in Mallorcean, a language with which I was not familiar, and then stormed from the bar. I followed at a discreet distance- he was still playing hell with his employee. Pablo made a telephone call from reception then filled me in on what the receptionist should have done. Evidently it was common practice in Spain, that if a death occurred on a Sunday, you always contacted a friendly doctor who diagnosed the patient as ill, not dead, and let him call the ambulance. Even if the 'patient' was demonstrably dead there was nothing the ambulance men could do about it because they had no authority to question a doctor.

So that is what Pablo had just done. He had called his friendly doctor, a Doctor Roca; however, it was going to take him some time to get there because he was still out with his family. So Pablo and I got down to some business for the next couple of hours until the doctor turned up.

'Do you want us to bring him downstairs again?' Pablo asked the doctor, after explaining the problem. The doctor shook his head. 'No, we'll let the ambulance men do that. That's what they get paid for. I've already called them so they should be here soon.'

When they arrived it was the same two men as earlier. They argued with the doctor when he insisted they had misdiagnosed the patient and they were now to take him to the hospital, but they were forced to comply. Everyone went upstairs to the widow's bedroom, including, I might add, the widow herself, who had not been told what the new procedure was all about. A quick examination of the body followed and the doctor declared the deceased alive and suffering from a heart attack! That bloody stupid consejeria then went and told her that as her husband was now no longer dead the ambulance was taking him to the hospital. She fell to her knees and began giving thanks to God 'for His infinite mercy'. The ambulance men, meanwhile, had discovered that rigor mortis was setting in, and kept shaking their heads when the doctor insisted that the condition was perfectly normal with some heart attack patients.

Then the pantomime began again. If it had proved difficult manoeuvring a newly dead body up a narrow Spanish hotel staircase, getting the same one down again, now stiffening considerably with rigor mortis was virtually impossible. The ambulance men dropped him twice, while the deceased's loyal wife insisted on assuring her dead husband he was going to be all right. The foolish woman actually believed he was still alive! 'You'll be all right, Henry,' she kept saying, at the same time stroking his dead cheek. 'Once they get you to hospital you're going to be fine.' I couldn't really understand why Pablo or the doctor didn't enlighten her, until Pablo explained later that had he done so the deception would have been uncovered and then the doctor would be in all sorts of trouble. So they had to allow the poor woman to accompany the ambulance to the hospital still believing her husband was alive and had a chance of recovering!

What a bloody experience that was, and it underlines the point that Spanish medical facilities in those times were nothing short of farcical.

Vincent Cobb

CHAPTER NINETEEN

1964 LATE SEASON 'TAKEOVERS'

During the high season of '64 we received sudden notification from the Spanish authorities that they were introducing an Airport Departure Tax. It wasn't an exorbitant charge but tour operators challenged it because of the lack of notice and also the lateness of the timing. It was to no avail, so we then had to go through the process of informing all of our passengers prior to departure that as this constituted government action we would have to hold them responsible for the charge. All the tour operators agreed and, at the time; none of the passengers objected.

A couple of weeks or so after this, I was called to Palma airport one day by Nuria, our Head Rep, who was having problems with a group of four clients, who were flatly refusing to pay the airport tax, insisting that it was our responsibility. I asked them if they had received the company's letter informing them of the change and they confirmed that they had. I then, once again, took them through the procedures in instances like this; they sat there impassively until I had finished and then repeated their stance that they disagreed and that it was definitely our responsibility to pay. Furthermore, they threatened not to check in for the flight until we agreed. Again I tried to reason with them but they were adamant. So I instructed the head rep. to close the flight. They went absolutely ape-shit, insisting that I had no right to do that. Finally I informed them that I was the Managing Director of the Company and not only had I every right, but that it was too late since I had just done it.

They got the message. I left them sitting on their suitcases in the lounge of Palma Airport totally dumbstruck. As I explained to the rep, I had no conscience about it as they had been given every opportunity to co-operate and had refused to do so. Anyway, they had already delayed the flight a half an hour. I also added for good measure, that as we had a very young George Best travelling on the flight. I believe he was only seventeen at the time, but already gaining stardom at Manchester United so we could hardly hold up the flight any longer. Of course we heard from their solicitors upon their return by scheduled service but, as our company solicitors quickly convinced them, they had no case whatsoever. Towards the end of September another Caledonian Airways DC7Cs was involved in an accident. This time the aircraft undershot the runway at Istanbul Airport. Fortunately there was only one injury, but the plane was a total write off, and served to remind us again of the industry's vulnerability.

It was also the year that our son was born and this time I was actually at home. In fact I was watching the election results being announced on television, on the night of October the 16th; he was born almost at the exact moment of Harold Wilson coming to power, although I could hardly blame him for that! What I used to refer to after that as the 'Good News' and the 'Bad'! 1964 was also the year of the beginning of the take-overs. Global Tours, a then subsidiary of GUS, began an aggressive expansionist programme and swallowed up Sunflight, leaving Doug Ellis to return to MAITO, the Midlands tour operator he shared with two other partners. It was towards the end of the year and into the next, when, to everyone's amazement, The Thomson Organisation, the newspaper group, bought out Ted Langton of Skytours, then the country's largest tour operator. This was followed very quickly by the takeover of a London tour operator, Riviera Holidays. Riviera was owned and run by Aubrey Morris, an ex-taxi driver who had become one of the travel industry's smaller entrepreneurs. What we were all unable to understand was why on earth Ted Langton had decided to sell. Skytours was a very successful company that, as I have already mentioned, had invested substantial sums of money into the developing Spanish resorts. One resort in particular worth commenting on was Calla Millor in the North Eastern part of Majorca. When Skytours 'discovered' the resort there was little or nothing there, other than an attractive beach. By now, it had become the most modern of all the Spanish resorts with a host of brand new, up to date hotels, each one having private facilities and entertainment amenities. It was the resort that during one winter period in the sixties hosted the Beatles and the Maharishi of Transcendental Meditation fame, together with his followers. Over six thousand people attended, which will give you an idea of the resort's phenomenal growth in such a short time span. Mind you, I have to add that they almost froze to death as none of the hotels had any central heating!

Ted Langton had by now completed the re equipping and renaming of his airline. It was now Britannia Airways of Luton, and boasted a fleet of fairly modern - at least comparatively speaking- Britannia aircraft. So, self-evidently, he was planning for the future. So why sell out? It was only later that we discovered that as visionary as Ted was, he was pretty clueless when it came to financial matters. It was said that he used to calculate his brochure selling prices on the back of a cigarette packet; he argued later, rightly or wrongly, that Thomson's had cheated him because of his lack of financial controls. Apparently, according to Ted, their accountants had pretty well torn his company apart, financially, discovered exactly how much it was worth, and then proceeded to 'screw' him by knowingly undervaluing it.

He became a very bitter man and, having been appointed Chief Executive of Thomson's new travel group, he decided they should be made to pay for their 'deception'. Ted's way of achieving this was to 'borrow' a million pounds or more of Thomson's' money out of the cash flow to complete a hotel he was in the process of building in Majorca. The hotel in question was the Arenal Park, a six hundred-bed monster. When the misfeasance came to light, as was inevitable, Ted was summarily dismissed from his position with Thomson's, but on the day of his departure he still managed to transfer a further three hundred thousand pounds to enable him to furnish the hotel. Also, what was not known at the time was that crafty old Ted had signed a long-term contract between his hotel and Skytours, charging outrageously high daily rates and committing the company to guaranteeing one hundred per cent bed occupancy throughout the tenure of the seven-year contract. As Ted commented at the time, borrowing an old quote: 'Revenge is sweeter on a cold plate.'

As an adjunct to the saga, a few years later, the Thomson Organisation was forced to buy the hotel Arenal Park from Ted Langton because of the onerous commercial conditions. I had the job of completing the take-over of the Arenal Park as, by then, I was responsible for the Overseas Thomson Hotels.

The Northern based tour operators, such as us, felt distinctly uneasy about the entry of these large organisations into our industry. In some ways the development was regarded as an intrusion; many of the smaller travel agents looked upon it as the breakup of the 'family'. Privately our concern had more to do with our ability to survive in what was becoming more and more a battle between the giants in our marketplace. On the performance side it had been a very good year for Gaytours. If we added the passenger figures for Luxitours, the new brand, we carried a total of just over forty thousand clients that summer, making us the largest tour operator in the North of England. Towards the end of the season, as we were finalising our programmes for the following year, we received an approach from the Thomson Organisation to purchase our companies. Without question it was something we had to give serious consideration to, not merely because of the attractiveness of the offer, but also because of our limited resources at a time when we realised that to remain competitive, which meant continued growth, substantial investment would be required. However, we refused to be hurried and so delayed our decision until early in the following year. The programme we mounted for 1965 was extravagant in the extreme. We coupled it with more exposure on Granada Television and arranged for one of the

Coronation Street stars to join us in promoting our product.

CHAPTER TWENTY

1965 THE END OF OUR FREEDOM

The booking season started very well for us that year, with exceptionally high demand for our holidays. A further innovation for us was the introduction for the first time ever of the 'fan jet' on package tours. In addition to our BEA Vanguard flights, which we had considerably expanded for '65, we had negotiated with BEA for the Trident aircraft to undertake a small series to Palma. It was an almost immediate sell-out; there was also considerable spin off for the remainder of our holidays due to our enhanced reputation in the industry. They were halcyon days. Load factors on all of our flights were encouraging, yet we still could not escape the growing feeling of isolation; we were lacking the consummate strength of the 'big boys' with all their resources.

There was a further and equally worrying development threatening to emerge within the industry in the spring of that year. The Association of British Travel Agents, or ABTA, as it was commonly referred to, that elitist body who until now had represented only that select group of travel agents who happened to possess what was known as an IATA Licence (a licence permitting the sale of air tickets for the world's national carriers who made up the member companies of IATA) was proposing major changes to the retail side of the industry, which if adopted, would make that organisation a significant player. The following is an outline of the proposals:

1) That in future ALL travel agents would have to become members of ABTA in order to trade.

2) All package tour operators would have to become members of ABTA if they wished to sell their holidays through the ABTA retail travel agents.

3) All tour operators would have to take out a bond with ABTA in order to safeguard clients' holidays in the future. ABTA's rationale was that the state of bankruptcies among tour operators, which had caused considerable distress amongst clients, especially those who had been stranded abroad, was also bringing the industry into disrepute and had to be addressed.

They had a point but our argument was 'what the hell gave this small elitist association the right to monopolise our industry?' A number of companies, ourselves included, objected to the proposals on the grounds of restraint of trade. I recall that one of the principal protagonists at the time was Wings, a small up market Tour Company, which also happened to be a member of ABTA. In brief, this small, and also elitist company, was effectively seeking to implement a 'closed shop' similar to those that many of the trade unions were imposing on companies at the time. Unknown to us, the scheme had the backing of the Labour government and was being supported behind the scenes by Roy Mason, then Minister of Trade and Industry. In other words, it was a stitch-up! ABTA had called a special convention of its members that spring, to be held in Jersey. As Luxitours was already a member company, Norman and I were qualified to attend. Those of us who did object were shouted down by a pre rehearsed concert party; the clincher came with the attendance and speeches at the convention of both Sir Isaac Woolfson, Chairman of Great Universal Stores, the owning company of Global Tours, and Roy Mason himself, who then openly supported the scheme.

It was a fait accompli decided upon by a small elitist group without allowing the non-members even the opportunity of a voice in the matter. Our view at the time was that the move had all the hallmarks of an illegal restraint; I still personally feel that had it been challenged in the courts it would have been deemed to be an illegal act. Nevertheless, it went through, and the timetable was for introduction the following year, giving companies like us one season to either accept the inevitable or to try to make some alternative arrangements. In the event of us deciding to go it 'alone' we felt we would well and truly be out in the cold.

But in the meantime we still had a programme to operate for that summer season. Unfortunately it got off to yet another sad start. I happened to be back in Jersey in the April when a DC3 aircraft, belonging to British United, crashed short of the runway killing all thirty passengers and crew. I didn't seem to be able to ignore these awful tragedies and I was always deeply affected by them. I remember leaving the island a few days later feeling very down, unable to stop myself thinking of the terror those people must have felt in the final moments before disaster struck. I am not sure if I ever got over all of those tragedies; it didn't stop me from flying probably because I was born with this inherent sense of stupidity.

The intensity of the season didn't let up for a moment. I continued to commute the hundred miles a day between Blackpool and Manchester when I happened to be in England. I still had to spend a great deal of the summer months in Europe negotiating hotel contracts, something again that was becoming increasingly difficult because of the competition and the struggle for an almost static supply of beds in an expanding market. Back in Manchester we had enhanced our management structure to cope with the growth of the business. By promoting Roger Corkhill, Norman's son, as Operations Manager, in charge of all flight operations, passenger manifests, and airport representation. I, rather like Norman himself, in my own case became something of a mentor to Roger, training him in all aspects of the tour industry. He went on to enjoy a very successful career in travel, eventually Retiring as Managing Director of Cosmos Tours.

We had continued negotiations with ICL the Computer Company for the installation of the 1901 System and preparations were underway to convert the necessary floor space. I 'leaned on' ICL a little to let us have one of their computer experts, a very talented young woman called Anne Beswick, to work on the installation. It actually took most of the summer to complete but we did have the advantage of providing some of our staff with on the ground training on the new system. Shortly after the completion of the new system I persuaded her to join us in an executive position to oversee the whole administration system.

At the height of the summer I happened to be in a resort called Lido di Jesolo, in Italy, being entertained in an up-market restaurant to a sumptuous dinner by our local agent. There must have been twenty five or thirty of us there that evening. When I asked Agostino what was the occasion for the celebration he laughingly informed me it was because, 'Tomorrow, Vincenzo, we declare our bankruptcy! So we celebrate with our creditors' money.' That was one of the idiosyncrasies I loved about the Italians, the ability to laugh at their own misfortunes. And the crazy thing was when I expressed some concern about who was going to represent us from then on, he proceeded to assure me I had nothing to worry about because the following week they would be starting another company.

CHAPTER TWENTY-ONE

1965/66 Development of the Industry

The next morning there was a telex from Norman waiting for me in the office of the 'bankrupt' agents, to the effect that I should return to England as soon as possible as Thomson's had more or less given him an ultimatum about purchasing the companies. Norman met me at Manchester Airport and we went off to a nearby hotel to discuss the issue. The options were quite clear; we could continue as we were, outside of ABTA, and face inevitable extinction; we could join ABTA and hope we would survive against the onslaught of the major operators; or we could 'bite the bullet' and sell out. Evidently Thomson's were pushing for a decision within the next couple of days, certainly no later than the end of the week. I owned ten per cent of the company so I had a fairly decisive role in the decision. Norman was quite a lot older than me and understandably he wanted out. As for myself, I wasn't yet thirty, still relatively young, and therefore not as anxious as Norman. I suggested we let them sweat for a while and see if they would improve their offer. They in fact did so. Norman went back to Thomson's informing them he was having difficulty in persuading me and as a result they had a 'private' meeting with me to increase the purchase price and at the same time offer me the job of Managing Director for the whole of the North of England and Scotland. Naturally I was highly flattered, especially with the salary, which was just about treble what dear Norman was paying me! I did the responsible thing and asked them to leave it with me for twenty- four hours. I had already discussed it with my wife and we had decided to accept. It was a considerable offer but it didn't prevent me lamenting the loss of my freedom. We accepted the offer and completed the deal that week. We also became a member of ABTA much to the relief of our Northern Travel Agents. I was coming under pressure from my friends in the Travel Industry, namely, Cliff Jones of Eccles Travel, Harry Langley of P&M Travel of Liverpool, (Now sadly deceased) Ronnie Booth of Aintree Travel, Stan McGowan of St. Helens (Also Deceased) – I could go on naming all of them, there were so many, but there were hundreds of them so I have only named those who I was closest to as friends.

A matter of weeks later Norman took himself off to London and I became a Career Executive. Nothing would ever be the same again, but isn't that life? At first I didn't really enjoy the appointment – it was strange being accountable, not just for the responsibility I had assumed but for the whole ambit of it; the North of England and for Scotland. Also, because of the sale and my new duties, the family moved to a nice house in Gatley, in Cheshire; it was a wrench leaving Blackpool but at least I was only twenty-minutes away from the office. After the take-over we rented the next door shop on Deansgate and integrated Skytours in there; so we were now selling the whole range of Manchester Holidays.

In 1965 Ringway opened the new building, so we had exceptional facilities upon which to develop the business, together with all of the hotels that Ted Langton had helped to build and of which we took advantage. All of our flying was now done by Britannia Airways.

I lived in Manchester for almost six years; we had a number of friends and the children were happy. As I was a firm Manu fan I got to see a lot of the home games, when I wasn't travelling abroad. In May of 1966 we went to Spain with Harry Langley and his family and stayed at one of Gabriel Escarrer's new hotels in C'an Pastilla, the Alexander. There we were introduced to Roger Hunt who played for Liverpool – Harry, by the way, was a Liverpool fanatic. We got on well with Roger and his wife but little did we know he would be playing for England the next month and winning the World Cup.

That was the time the site for one of our hotels was blasted with dynamite to start the foundations. Moe of that later.

In 1966 Roger Corkhill and myself began organising overseas trips for the Man U supporters clubs. It was a great success and it was followed by Harry Langley doing the same thing for the Liverpool fans. We both of us made arrangements to go on each of the trips and we had a great time of it (we also made a lot of money.)

Then I had a call from Sir Matt Busby who wanted a favour from me; I obliged and we became great friends after that; I remember Sheena, his daughter, very well and the only sad thing was that I was unable to go Matt's funeral as I was in hospital. But each week or so Matt left me two tickets for the Directors box. I took my son on a couple of occasions and we met some of the celebrities, including Mat Munroe. I was quite enjoying myself in Manchester; I played golf with a number of the Travel Agents and we negotiated for the rental of large premises in the centre of the City. The new computer system worked very well and everything was under control.

CHAPTER TWENTY-TWO

THE THOMSON YEARS

I have deliberately drawn an 'anecdotal' line under the package tour industry at the year 1965, not because I believed that that was the time when it reached maturity, but more because my life, on the whole, began to take on a less dramatic shape than hitherto. The coming of age of the industry certainly didn't happen overnight; in fact, as is the case with all new entities, it evolved slowly, almost ponderously, rather like the growth of a child. In other words the industry didn't suddenly throw out all those ancient aircraft or transform all hotel accommodation into four-star units. Nor did most companies abandon the quill pen and ink, the common method of processing the administration requirements. The truth is that at that time its development was probably no further advanced than adolescence. What was manifestly changing was the 'player.' In the place of the mavericks, people like my old boss, if you will, national well resourced, and well respected companies were now underpinning us, and if the industry stood any chance of reaching maturity it could only be achieved with the backing of these substantial institutions. Some of the original entrepreneurs hung on, either through stubbornness or because there were no attractive offers on the table for their companies. But rather like the dinosaurs, their demise, sooner or later, was inevitable. Mind you, as a kind of entrepreneur myself, I survived much longer than they did.

We went into 1966 with a totally reshaped countenance. The Skytours offices in Manchester were closed and the operations absorbed into those of Gaytours on Deansgate. That in turn required us to enhance the new computer system, almost before it went on line, to accommodate the additional capacity. Aside from retaining a couple of flights with BEA on the Vanguard and the Trident the flying programme was progressively transferred to Britannia Airways as I have already said. It was a year of phenomenal sales as growth continued unabated; the new integrated group was already making its presence felt in the North. In many ways, my job became easier as functions were consolidated into London. My travelling programme, initially, was considerably reduced as more and more large hotel units began to come on stream, and London was taking care of most of the contracting.

One of the problems we encountered with the pace of hotel expansion in Spain was the number of questionable builders that came out of the woodwork. For instance, a very large hotel under construction in Pineda, a Costa Brava resort, collapsed killing three workmen. Another fell to the ground in Majorca when it had reached only three stories. In other cases hotel construction commenced in a wave of optimism, only to be abandoned when the already inadequate financial resources dried up. So I began travelling again, dissatisfied with the lack of expertise apparent in London. I decided arbitrarily, whether London liked it or not, that I would retain responsibility for hotel contracting for both Gaytours and Luxitours; as it happened the contracting staff in London were fully involved in attempting to resolve their own problems and were grateful for the assistance.

Their administrative systems for example were stretched to breaking point. London did not have the benefit of an up to date computer installation and trying to merge Skytours' operations with those of Riviera Holidays was proving to be a chronic nightmare. The company was also without the benefit of a suitable Chief Executive. Following the speedy departure of Ted Langton, Thomson's was obliged, in the short term, to give the job to Aubrey Morris, the ex-owner of Riviera. Aubrey was a nice man who was very well intentioned but totally out of his depth at this level. So things went from bad to worse and breakdowns began to occur in administration; hotel rooming lists were not sent out on time and more often than not were inaccurate. Flight manifests suffered a similar fate, so much so that Britannia Airways could never rely on accurate load - factor information. Invoices were proving to be an even bigger disaster; either they did not turn up at the right travel agent or when they did, they were incomplete and inaccurate. The one thing the group was sitting on, and the one aspect, which we learned later, had encouraged Thomson's and other national companies to invest in the industry, was cash flow: the vast flow of income that came from clients settling their bills eight weeks prior to departure as the contracts stipulated together with the delay in settling hotel invoices. It was an immense source of income and Thomson's insisted, almost under penalty of death, that we chased 'The Money'. While this administrative debacle was going on in London I managed to isolate us in the North of England and operate at a high level of efficiency.

It was pointed out to me some years later that evidently I had become, unwittingly, a case study in vertical integration at the London Business School. I was highlighted as the executive who prevented Thomson's achieving total integration in London because I refused to compromise my independence. It is a pity that the London Business School never took the trouble to converse with me about the matter. I would have told them that they were probably right about my resisting attempts to merge the Northern operation with that of London but certainly not for the reasons they stated. The reality was that London had become a citadel of gross inefficiency and it was clearly out of the question that they could absorb our by now significant operation without causing a total collapse of the whole enterprise. There was a standard joke at the time that I always felt was very apposite. It was said amongst the executives that if you happened to be away from the office sick for any particular week you could consider yourself fortunate because you might well have been forced to accept the position of Chief Executive! We had a veritable stream of them.

The easier life I had anticipated failed to materialise. It was true that I was no longer commuting from Blackpool because during the previous winter I had contracted viral pneumonia and had to be hospitalised for three weeks (But for that I might well have found myself as Chief Executive!). So, as I said, the family moved to Manchester. But despite this, my bi-weekly sessions in London apart, I was actually doing as much travelling as I had ever done on the hotel contracting side. But that was the year in which England won the World Cup and optimism was rife.

The Wilson administration was giving the trade unions pretty well what they asked for so everyone was happy. However, with a majority in Parliament of only three, the Prime Minister decided to call a premature general election the following year; the Labour Party was then voted back into office with an increased majority. And that was when our problems in the travel industry really began. One of Wilson's/Healey's first acts was devaluation of the pound. Remember that infamous Wilson statement that the 'Pound in your pocket won't be worth any less'?

Holiday prices went up immediately and substantially because we were unable to purchase foreign currency at anywhere near the same price as pre-devaluation. This affected not only all hotel prices but also the flight cost because airlines had always dealt in dollars for the fuel element, together with the normal administrative costs we incurred abroad in the course of our business. As if that were not enough, Wilson then decided to introduce strict foreign exchange-control regulations and we were faced with the fifty-pound limit.

In essence that meant that all clients wishing to take foreign holidays were restricted to taking no more than fifty pounds per person out of the country on departure. The regulatory procedure was the 'pink form' that every person had to complete at the time of booking. It was an Administrative nightmare and in the end became impossible to enforce. In fact had it not been for the passive goodwill of the holidaymakers the law would have been superfluous; I cannot imagine any government being allowed to get away with it today.

I remember one day that summer going to the Bank of England to ask them how they policed the system. An official took me down into a basement room where there were literally hundreds of thousands, if not millions, of 'pink forms' stacked everywhere. Not one single form had even been given a glance!

In a way the travel industry became something of a, scapegoat' for the Labour administration. We were besieged with strangulatory regulations, which appeared to us to be designed to discourage people from taking foreign holidays. For instance, it was not a straightforward matter of paying our hotel bills when they were due; effectively we had to request permission from the Bank of England to remit the funds for every single invoice. We metaphorically shouted and screamed at officialdom gone mad but it was to no avail. Nobody listened and our overhead costs were rising astronomically. But we managed to struggle through the summer, bloodied but not beaten!

There were ways of beating the restriction on currency. One was to hide monies in your suitcase, and the other was to find someone who lived offshore who had no restrictions.

At the time I was negotiating with Antonio, our Mallorcan Agent to build a Hotel in Arenal. He put up some money and arranged for Thomsons to 'Invest' a fair amount of money in a forward hotel contract. The hotel we named the Caribbean; it was going well in construction but, unfortunately, we ran out of money.

So I travelled to Jersey to see my old friend Walter Collins and asked him if he might be interested in investing. I showed him the figures and he almost immediately said yes; so we were saved – or at least Thomson's money was. The hotel opened on time and the passengers arrived, but then we had to close it because it was too cold. I noticed the swimming pool was about a quarter the size of an Olympic Pool.

That was 1966

CHAPTER TWENTY-THREE

THE LATER YEARS
THE FAN-JET

In 1967 Jed Williams, the then Managing Director of Britannia Airways, submitted a detailed technical paper to the Thomson Organisation regarding the question of future aircraft requirements. It was incredibly complex, particularly for people like the travel executives who had no knowledge whatsoever of aircraft technicalities, and contained a great deal of specifics from the Boeing Aircraft Company in relation to the Boeing 737 jet, one of the new short haul generation of fan jet aircraft. Jed Williams had clearly studied the acquisition of the plane for the short and medium term replacement of the ageing Britannia aircraft. I imagine the shock for the organisation was the sums that Jed was calculating, which literally soared into the millions. I believe that was the moment of truth, for the Thomson Organisation's commitment to the travel industry, and in a way for the whole future of the industry. There is an old maxim in business, that companies either progress or they regress; that they simply cannot stand still, which is really what we and the rest of the industry was trying to do. In the event, and to their credit,

Thomson's took the plunge and approved the purchase of three Boeing 737 aircraft, thus inciting the largest financial investment ever before seen by a package tour operator.

However, before the order could be definitely placed we first had to seek the approval of our old 'friends' the Labour government, not an easy task given that the 737 was the aircraft with which BEA was seeking to replace the Vanguard and the BAC111 on short haul routes. This became a political matter between the organisation and the government. I don't suppose we will ever really know the truth of how it came about but, to our collective astonishment, approval was granted to us and refused for BEA. Furthermore BEA was instructed as a nationalised industry that they had to purchase more of the BACIII aircraft as the replacement for the Vanguards and the Viscounts.

It was fully a year and a half before the first of the 737s came into service for Britannia. I recall very clearly joining the inaugural flight to Dubrovnik with Lord Thomson and the rest of the Thomson hierarchy. We were met at Dubrovnik Airport by a welcoming committee and a team of national dancers. Poor Lord Thomson was unable to escape them, even when we went down the coast to Budva the dancers followed. And while we were all entertaining ourselves in the local casino (believe it or not limited gambling was permitted in Tito's Yugoslavia), Lord Thomson was 'stuck' with the dance group for more than three hours!

But it truly was a momentous occasion and marked the beginning of the new generation of package tour aircraft. Not too long after that other private airlines found the funding to re-equip their fleet, those that did not, or could not, eventually went to the wall.

Another tragic accident happened during this period, this time to one of the companies which were still operating our coach/air programme to Jersey: Derby Aviation, now known as British Midland since the opening of the new Castle Donington Airport. During the summer of '67, I was at my home close to Manchester Airport one Sunday afternoon, when I received a call from one of the Operations staff at Ringway, informing me that a Derby Aviation aircraft, one of the old Argonauts I have written so much about, was in serious trouble, and was circling the airport over Stockport. The next call I got was to tell me that the plane in question had come down in the middle of a housing estate on the outskirts of Stockport; I was asked if I could go along and try to lend some assistance if there were any surviving passengers.

I arrived some ten minutes later and to my absolute horror I saw the aircraft had somehow crash-landed on some waste ground immediately in between three blocks of flats. It was already burning fiercely by the time I got there; I could actually see, through the aircraft windows, passengers still trapped in their seats. How the pilot had been able to avoid crashing into one of the buildings I will never know. It was one of the most horrifying and traumatic tragedies I have ever, or will ever, witness. Those poor, unfortunate people were completely unable to move, or in any way help themselves, as a result of the broken limbs they had suffered during the crash landing. The only survivor was the pilot; everyone else was burned to death.

British Midland was eventually purchased by Michael Bishop (now Sir Michael). I first met Michael at Ringway Airport in the old days when he was working for Derby Aviation on the Operations side. I don't believe either of us realised at the time just what an aviation empire he would go on to build. But like the package tour industry itself, there was no overnight miracle in the airline sector. Most of the old aircraft in service during the early sixties were still operational towards the end of that decade. They included the DC4 s, the Argonauts, and even the DC3 s and Vikings. And accidents with charter aircraft were still occurring, albeit on a very much reduced scale.

Britannia Airways suffered a disaster when a Britannia came down at Ljubljana in Yugoslavia, killing all on board, and a Court Line plane crashed on its approach to Barcelona Airport, again with no survivors. That was also the season when over bookings on the Costa Brava had become horrific, with the same culprits who had been responsible for the situation in the previous years. I sadly recall that as soon as the news of the Court Line crash filtered through to the resorts the couriers invaded the Clarkson's Hoteliers (The Tour Company whose passengers were on board) to negotiate for the vacancies the deaths had incurred. It wasn't until we were into the seventies that Thomson's was able to replace all of their Britannia aircraft with modem 737 jets and we saw the transition from piston engine aircraft to fan jets.

In 1967 Antonio and I commissioned the building of a second hotel in Mallorca; this was to be called the Antigua constructed across the road from the Caribbean; I'm sure Antonio made a mistake here because it was supposed to be named after the Caribbean Island – Antigua. Again Thomson's 'Invested' a large deposit and construction was underway. However, we also, predictably, ran out of funds, and we had to call on the help from Walter Collings. Some of his funds went via Norman Corkhill; he spirited away some forty thousand pounds in his suitcase but when he arrived in Mallorca the money was missing. How that happened we will never know but we never found the money.

In any event the Antigona opened on schedule and was filled very quickly. Norman had to replace the missing money from his own resources.

What a tragedy!

The Package Tour Industry

CHAPTER TWENTY-FOUR

NOTHING NEW UNDER THE SUN

1968 was the year someone seemed intent on killing me; I was shot at, first in Krakow and then in Cyprus. That was the year when we began organising trips abroad for Manchester United football fans and as a committed supporter I made a point, when I was able, of going on the flight. We also began the Saturday Night's out in Hamburg; eight pounds only we charged and we couldn't get enough aircraft to fill all the demand. Eventually we had to cancel all of the flights because the Hamburg Authorities wouldn't allow our planes to land at the airport. Some of the clients behaviour was absolutely disgusting, and I was rather glad to we had to abandon the trips.

However, back to the Manchester United excursions. The Krakow trip was when Man U played the return leg against a club called Gornic, in Silesia. It also happened to coincide with student riots in the city that erupted because the communist authorities had begun publicly burning books. Unintentionally I found myself caught in the middle of the riots among a group of students when the police, finding the water cannons somewhat ineffective, started shooting at us with live bullets. A young female student standing next to me was hit in the shoulder by a bullet, which I was sure was intended for me. I rather think they considered me to be one of the organisers.

On the way to the football match we made a slight diversion to visit Auschwitz, the hellhole of a concentration camp created by the Nazis. It was an experience never to be forgotten either by myself or anyone else on that coach. Aside from a guided tour of the camp, which included the gas chambers and the ovens, we were invited by the Russian official to stand outside, in one of the squares, for just five minutes. It was March and it was very cold and despite being dressed in overcoats, scarves, woolly hats, and gloves, we were soon frozen. The guide then reminded us that when the camp was operational the inmates had had to stand outside, as we were, with little clothing, for up to twelve hours. If any one of them moved, they were shot! It was a very humbled group who left the camp that day.

Later in the year I was asked to go to Beirut to speak with a partner of Lord Thomson's in the country's television station. It was uneventful but I do remember my wife and I commenting on what a lovely city Beirut was. Of course that was years before the 'troubles' started, although we were asked if we wouldn't mind touring one of the Palestinian refugee camps. It was a hell of an eye opener and you couldn't help sympathising with people having to live in such squalid conditions.

There was no sewage, very little drinking water, and the people was having to exist on scraps of food. Our hearts went out to them. But later I was informed these were refugees from the old Palestine before it became Israel in 1948 and according to the Israelis they could have been accommodated in the new country.

From Beirut we flew over to Cyprus for a few days at the invitation of a travel agent in Famagusta. Today that would probably equate with offering the Iraqis long weekend breaks in Tel Aviv! We stayed at one of the beachside hotels in Famagusta, occupied in the main by United Nations' peacekeeping forces, and enjoyed a couple of days in the sunshine. However, one morning, on our way to visiting an ancient Greek shrine, I noticed a couple of men pointing rifles at us. The next thing they opened fire and bullets actually pierced the bodywork of the taxi carrying us, just missing the guide. The Greeks, had attacked, unknown to us, a Turkish Cypriot village the night before killing thirteen of the inhabitants. As we happened to be the closest target and obviously not Turks, they were seeking revenge. On the way back to the airport at Nicosia we were provided with a special escort; I believed at the time it was because of the tension between the Turkish and Greek populations. I had to smile when I was informed that we had inadvertently become caught up in the transfer of General Grivas, a targeted terrorist, who was in the process of transfer to the airport following his arrest. It was time to go home! I reported to Lord Thomson that discussions had gone well with his partner and he was prepared to buy him out for a reasonable sum.

Towards the end of the sixties I became the Chairman of the North West Committee of ABTA, the Association of British Travel Agents. One of my duties at the time was to appear on Granada Television to speak on behalf of the industry. It was an interesting little adventure if only because it was something different; it was also 'live' television. I made a number of appearances on the show at that time but it quickly became obvious that the real purpose of the program was to publicly embarrass our industry by attempting to highlight (even exaggerate!) the volume of complaints from clients. I am rather glad to say that I was able to defend the industry robustly and I didn't really mind because each week I was treated to a steak and kidney pie in the studio's canteen!

In 1968 Antonio and I began our third hotel in Magalluf. This was to be called the Honolulu and this time we had planned to fund the development almost with sufficient resources. Again, Walter Collings came to the rescue; so did Thomsons. As far as they were concerned they were funding the development of hotels – exactly as Ted Langton did and his successor did – to arrange long-term contracts with favourable terms. So we were satisfying all of the parties.

However, after the Honolulu opened we at Thomson began the £18 three night holiday in the winter; £20 if you wanted an extra night. It was a revolution in the travel industry and we sold out almost immediately. I recall very well at the Board Meeting when we decided to embark on the cheap winter short-breaks, that pretty well all of us gave the Thomson Main Board an ultimatum: Either they got rid of the current Managing Director or we would resign en-masse. The guy in charge, who was married to an American woman with a broad Bronx accent, and who had no experience whatsoever, resigned that week.

The following year, Antonio was beset with greed. What he tried to do was to split the parties; in other words he wanted the three hotels for himself and to achieve this he mortgaged them up to the hilt with debt through a local banker who was the Godfather to one of his children. Walter had run out of funds and Norman was the same. So I persuaded one of the accountants in London to transfer almost sixty-thousand pounds to the Honolulu; this pissed off Antonio no end; the mortgage was repaid. In addition, because I had a personal letter from Antonio asking us to transfer the money for the hotel bills through his Swiss Account; had I disclosed this to the Spanish Authorities he would definitely have gone to prison.

So he succumbed. The three of us got the Honolulu and Antonio got the Caribbean and the Antigona. In the end it was a well worth venture although it affected Walter's nervous position because his wife had to section him in Jersey and he spent almost six months in the Psychiatric Hospital. I put the blame on Antonio and we never worked with him again.

CHAPTER TWENTY-FIVE

THE EARLY SEVENTIES

In 1970 I was asked to come to London to work on the next year's brochure. It was very hard work as I was told I would be responsible for the whole of the pricing for 1971. At the time we were facing up to the competition of Clarksons. This was a company that had started life in the Dutch Bulb fields and had then, under Tom Gullick, infiltrated into the overall package tour business. By the beginning of the seventies it had become a serious competitor and was threatening our existence as the main UK Tour Operator.

So I decided that this year would have to be 'Shit or Bust'. I priced the holidays on a 95% load factor; this was unheard of as the standard pricing formulae was pitched at only 90% load factor. It was a dangerous game and we had to get the approval of the main Thomson's Board before we could go ahead. Gordon Brunton, the chief executive of Thomson, accepted my formulae and we went ahead.

In 1971 we out-priced Clarksons and for them it was the beginning of the end. I was rewarded with a first class holiday, paid for in total by the Board. My wife and I flew, first to New York, where we spent a few days, and then on to

Jamaica where we stayed at the Half Moon Hotel in Montego Bay. We had a wonderful time there and coming home we stopped, first at Toronto and then on to Montreal. We flew back on the VC10 direct to Manchester.

In the middle of that year we - Thomson that is – moved premises to Greater London House with spacious accommodation, and I was asked to organise Travel Agents sessions in the North as Marketing had decided that we would trade under the name of Thomson rather than the three brands. They went off very well although I got my friends in the Industry to formulate a plan for keeping Gaytours; it didn't work but we had a hell of have a laugh.

That year I was also invited to move myself and the family to London – to do what? It wasn't mentioned. However, I insisted that to move me from Manchester they would have to appoint me a Deputy Managing Director under Bryan Llewellyn, the new Chief Executive. They refused – or rather Bryan Llewellyn did. He offered me a particular job in London, without mentioning what it would be, but I would still have the overall responsibility for the Northern Operation. With all of the pressures exerted on me I finally accepted.

In 1971 we moved into Kings Langley in Hertfordshire. As you can imagine the kids were upset although the house was very nice; we were also out of our depth financially as the prices in

London were outrageous. The day we moved into the house there was a letter pushed through the letter box, unstamped; it was from Bryan Llewellyn informing me that from now on I would have *no responsibility whatsoever for the Northern Operations,* but he did have a "Bit of a Job" for me at Head Office. I thought it was a disgrace; the cowardly Llewellyn didn't have the guts to warn me in advance, he waited until I had made the move to London, uprooted the family, and then surreptitiously dropped me in it! And the job he offered me was to take charge of the Thomson Hotels at a reduced salary from the one I was offered. Talk about Ted Langton being stitched up, it was nothing compared to the upheaval we had endured.

I had to accept the job even though we had very few hotels. There was a small one in Playa san Juan, close to Alicante; a second one was the Torredorada in Benidorm; there was also a small one close to the airport in Athens, where the King of Saudi Arabia stayed, and I think that was it. What a job that was, if anything it was humiliating but Llewellyn had forced me into a corner. I thought very much about Ted Langton and wondered how I might get revenge as he did.

At the time a hotel was under construction in Sicily; it was by the beach and not far from Palermo, and was owned by one of the Mafia bosses. Also, David Lewis, of Chelsea Girl, was building the Santa Lucia hotel in Palma Nova, in

Mallorca. Another monster hotel was under construction in Magalluf, the Magalluf Park hotel; Senor Mereno was the owner of that establishment and he came to me wanting to sell it. But I had no mandate so I passed him on to Frances Higgins, a nice enough guy but who was one of those dummies from Charterhouse School; and would you believe he was actually appointed Managing Director of Thomson Holidays. In the end he signed a 21-year lease to be paid in *Swiss Francs*; now do you believe he was a dummy? – so was Llewellyn for appointing him.

By then were ready to open the Mellehia Bay hotel in Malta. It was a magnificent hotel built by Ted Langton with some generous help from the Maltese Government. The whole of the Thomson Board came with us to the opening – other of course than Lord Thomson. That was when Bryan Llewellyn was appointed as Chief Executive. At the time I quite liked him until I discovered what a devious and manipulative bastard he really was, then I grew to mistrust him. That night at the Mellehia Bay myself and some of my travel mates, got as drunk as skunks and gave a melody in the disco. There was three or four of us, including Harry Langley and Stan McGowan; we emptied the place.

It was at that time I met up with Tony Hanson, a sharp-eyed lawyer who kept on reminding me he had been to Cambridge. He was doing the paperwork for David Lewis for the

Santa Lucia; it soon became apparent that – regardless of his background education – we had an awful lot in common. Over the years we did a lot of deals together but I'll come on to that later.

When the Magalluf Park opened I took charge of it and soon after Tony Hanson and I, with the background of the rent being in Swiss Francs, were able to sell it on to Vernon Ray, a Swiss rogue who was into takeovers. He was the one who made a number of enemies in Switzerland after taking over Bally Shoes and then tried to get rid of the Chairman who was on the board of Swissair. Nevertheless, Tony and I got the usual commission from the sale and Tony actually tied up a residual value in case Verna Ray wanted to sell it on. Like I said, Tony was a sharp-eyed lawyer.

The Santa Lucia opened on time and suddenly we had over three thousand beds to look after. So I re-organised. I brought in a marketing director; an accountant from Manchester, and Tony Neira, another sharp guy who was a Spaniard; he ran the catering side of the hotels and who inevitably shaved a bit off the top!

So there we were, based now in Watford and having the time of my life. I travelled quite a bit, mostly to Mallorca where we also had an office and then I got more involved with Gabriel Escarrer – he was the one who I mentioned earlier had broadened his base in the hotel industry. Now he was in trouble financially. He had bought the

Hotel Victoria, a five star hotel on the Paseo Maritimo and he had run out of money to pay off the balance. So he came to me and I went to Tony Hanson. Tony, by some means or another, arranged a down payment of some two million pounds. He was then left with a balance to find, within three months, of another three million pounds. That was fine but Tony did not have the wherewithal to find the money. So he came to me. As it happened Llewellyn had received a note from Gordon Brunton, the Thomson Chief Executive, that he had some millions available and could Llewellyn find a home for it.

So I jumped. Punched out a paper on the value of hotel investment and persuaded Llewellyn to part with the three million pounds to buy the Escarrer hotels. The Aquarium Hotel close to the beach in Palma Nova, The Trinidad and the Jamaica in Magaluf, and the Lido, on the beach, in Camp-de-Mar.

We met up with Escarrer who was by now desperate for the money to meet his payments; I remember him telling me that unless he received the balance in the next few days he would go bankrupt. Prior to this I discussed the matter with Tony and we both decided that we would place the three million pounds on deposit in the Bank of New York; it seemed a bit pointless in simply handing it over to Escarrer. Then we arranged a back- to- back inter-bank guarantee, so Gabriel could then arrange an immediate loan from the Bank of Bilbao. Of course he would have to pay the interest. He agreed and we left the money lying in New York until the day that the peseta devalued. We then had over three hundred thousand pounds. I asked John Gill, the Thomson financial director what we should do with the money; he didn't want to know, so he made Tony and I three hundred thousand pounds richer. And they actually thought I knew nothing about business? Tony even arranged, through his paperwork technique, a strong residual value in the hotels; in other words, were the hotels ever to be sold, Tony, and guess who the other partner was? A pretty large sum of money would be paid to the beneficiaries.

So now we had an empire with six hotels in Mallorca, two under construction in Portinaux in Ibiza, one under construction in Sicily, and the remaining others I mentioned earlier. In all we now had almost six thousand beds under my control, with the Saracen Sands in Sicily still to come on stream. I was also made a director of the Mellehia Bay Hotel in Malta and had to attend board meetings once a month.

At the end of that year, and the beginning of the next, Llewellyn and Frances Higgins bought out Sunflight. Personally, I thought it was a crazy idea as pretty well everyone in the travel business knew that Harry Goodman was on the verge of going bankrupt. We, in the Overseas Hotels, were stuck with some crazy hotel just outside of Rome.

We visited the place and discovered it had almost a hundred and thirty per cent occupancy during the day; at the weekend it was virtually deserted. When the manager told us that it was a Hooker's paradise I informed the board that with the advent of Suntours they hadn't engaged in vertical integration, this was now horizontal integration! That brought a laugh but we got rid of the hotel.

The year after that Harry Goodman started Intersun; then he kept insisting that "Small is Beautiful".

In the spring the Saracen Sands, a six hundred-bed unit, came on stream. It was a difficult negotiating phase because the owner refused us permission to include spring water wells in the grounds included in the contract when he had already agreed they could be included. I walked out on him and, through our lawyer he told me I had twenty-four hours to get off the Island. In the vernacular I informed him he could "F" off. Our lawyer, from Rome, told me I was crazy because man had the reputation of making people disappear.

I still wouldn't give in and made arrangements for the first group of passengers to be accommodated elsewhere. Finally, he was the one who gave in and the wells were reinstated.

Our first flight was almost due to depart but on the Island we had a group of our couriers on a training course. I got hold of the personnel director, who was in charge of the course, and insisted they would be couriers would have to start cleaning the hotel. A furious row broke out, I only got my way when I informed him that if the hotel wasn't cleaned then we would have to transfer the clients – already on their way – to an alternative hotel and he would get the blame. We opened on schedule.

Back to the water: Would you believe that after we had taken over the hotel the wells were poisoned with oil and became inaccessible. And guess whom we had to buy our water from? Di Bella, the owner who owned most of the water companies in that part of Sicily.

Some two months later I was invited to the opening ceremony. The Cardinal was there with all of his entourage, and of course Di Bella. This was also on local television and I was given a gift of a gold necklace; I gave it to my wife and she cherished that until it was stolen.

The Package Tour Industry

CHAPTER TWENTY-SIX

1973/1974 ONWARDS
PROMOTION TO THE RANKS

In October of 1973 Egypt and other of the Middle East countries, including Syria and Jordan, invaded Israel; initially it was called the Yom Kippur war. The result was that the middle - east was defeated heavily and one of the consequences was the forming of the oil Cartel, which immediately hiked prices by some 250%; this was right at the time we were launching our 1974 brochures so a policy of holiday surcharges was introduced. At the same time, Nixon, the American President, supplied Israel with up to date weapons; this caused a furore amongst the middle-eastern nations and prompted a recession both in the US and here in the UK. It was interesting that Edward Heath, the British Prime Minister supported Israel. In the winter of 1973 we had the 3-day working week together with shortages of electricity. Then, early in 1974 we had the miners' strike that went on for four weeks until a general election was called. Wilson got back into power and the first thing he did was to pay the miners whatever it was they wanted. Inflation hit us very hard in 1975 – it almost reached 26% a year and to satisfy the staff at headquarters we had to increase their wages by some two percent a month. This is what the Wilson Government was doing to us.

The Holiday business was suffering terribly with high oil prices, inflation, and heading towards a recession. At least by then we had gotten rid of the fifty- pound currency limit. But each of the companies faced exorbitant surcharges and we suffered a decline in passenger numbers.

Bryan Llewellyn called me to the office in the spring of 1974. I had no idea what he wanted and neither had he given me any information or advance warning. I already knew that with the Suntours acquisition they were already in a mess. For a while he waffled on in his inimitable style, then he asked me if I would be prepared to take over all of the Overseas activities. He even went as far as suggesting he might include Marketing. It was patently obvious that he had run out of patience with Frances Higgins; this man was evidently a very square peg in a very round hole.

So Bryan Llewellyn appointed me Joint Managing Director of Thomson Holidays with overall responsibility for the Overseas operations. In short, I was responsible for all of the reps, a chain of travel agents across Spain, coach companies, and a head office staff, which in turn required a move back to London.

I was given a very nice office. Privileged parking space, my own secretary, and nearby was the office of Norman Lewis, the contracts manager. In a way I couldn't believe this was happening to me, not after the deviousness of Bryan Llewellyn; perhaps he was becoming enlightened.

But that was the year of the unfinished hotels. We had various "Artists Impressions" in our brochure and Norman Lewis had made arrangements for a so-called builder to regularly inspect the growing number of establishments. Every week he sent the same kind of message after visiting each of the hotels in the various resorts: "If the present tempo of works continues then the hotel will be finished on schedule".

I don't believe he visited any of the hotels – so I sacked him and brought in a civil engineer who was recommended to me. He told us the truth, that not one single hotel would be finished on schedule. So, we were up the creek without the proverbial paddle. The hotel contractors had to find some alternative accommodation; more often than not it was in establishments that couldn't compare to the ones the clients may have booked. And the press headlines were all about this 'Summer of Discontent'.

I spent the rest of the summer still travelling; inspecting the unfinished hotels and trying to arrange, with our local senior staff, for alternative hotels; discussing matters with the local area managers; visiting our Spanish Travel agencies, and then flying to Athens.

That was the next time when anything was heard of Famagusta when its invasion by Turkey triggered off a war with Greece. One of the Famagusta resort hotel managers, who had worked for us in Malta at one time, was killed instantly by an air to ground missile fired indiscriminately by a Turkish fighter plane. Following the invasion the Greek authorities immediately announced a general militarization and 'call up' of all available young men. In effect that closed all of the tourist hotels and airports and since all coaches were instantly commandeered, overland transportation ground to a halt.

We at Thomson had approximately twenty thousand holidaymakers spread across mainland Greece and the islands at the time who required urgent repatriation to the UK. It was a complete disaster; no catering facilities at any hotel; no cleaning; no transport of any description, and no airports open to accept our repatriation aircraft. Needless to say we performed something of a miracle. In four days Greece had become bereft of tourist services. We brought coaches in from Yugoslavia and Italy, thanks to the assistance of the appropriate authorities, and transferred clients hundreds of miles to the nearest civil airports. We charted whole cruise and ferry ships out of ports such as Brindisi in Italy and sent them out to the Greek Islands to bring our clients home. At one stage we had to consider seriously providing emergency food aid to replenish the islands' stockpiles, although in the event it wasn't necessary as we brought in supplies on the coaches and the ships. Greece was at war with Turkey but our concern was for the welfare and safety of our twenty thousand clients. In the event not a single casualty was incurred and every passenger was brought home safely. It was four days of intense pressure and activity and naturally, as was usual in the travel industry, sleep again became a luxury. In Majorca, as I mentioned earlier, we completed the purchase of the Arenal Park Hotel from Ted Langton. That was less of a policy decision than a case of commercial necessity. As we were well into owning or leasing hotels I, together with Tony Hanson, persuaded David Lewis to buy the Honolulu, in Palma Nova. The sale price wasn't exactly exorbitant , but neither was it cheap, and Walter Collings and Norman made a lot of money; I didn't do too badly myself!

The night of the takeover I was in Switzerland awaiting the funds to be transferred, when I was informed a murder had occurred at the hotel. Evidently a body, fully clothed, was discovered lying on the hotel's patio and it was only when a post mortem was carried out, and of course the body was stripped, that the examiner discovered the knife wounds which were the cause of death. Apparently, the young man had been knifed to death in his nightclothes and then re-dressed and thrown from the bedroom balcony to make it look like an accident. A man was arrested on suspicion, but, since the matter involved foreigners, the Spanish police, under the Franco regime, didn't have the commitment to investigate further. And so it was dropped.

The same hotel experienced a very serious fire some time later and although there were no fatalities the hotel was closed for almost a year and cost around a quarter-of-a-million pounds to refurbish. Thomson's also constructed one of the industry's largest hotels during that same period: this was the Sahara Beach Hotel in Monastir, Tunisia. It could accommodate approximately two thousand people, and was built in partnership with the World Bank and a local Tunisian partner. The overall presentation of the hotel was quite superb. It was right on the beach, every room had its own bathroom and balcony and it boasted a variety of entertainment facilities including its own nightclub. Where it fell down was on its cleanliness, or rather, I should say, it's almost total lack of it. At any one time during the whole of that first summer, more than four hundred clients were ill with gastroenteritis. This went on for week after week; doctors were constantly visiting the hotel, and making money, and, in fact, at one stage we had to arrange for a regular in-house surgery.

When it appeared that there was no easy answer to this I arranged for a British team of hotel hygiene specialists to spend a week in the hotel. The bottom line was that generally they would rate hotel hygiene on a scale of nought to ten; the Sahara Beach, they informed me, wouldn't even find a place on the scale. It was that bad. They suggested that we should close it immediately as a potential death trap. Of course we couldn't do that, costs aside, it would have been impossible to organise alternative accommodation in the middle of summer. So we did the next best thing available to us; we closed down the area of the kitchens, where the problem was the worst and we opened an additional, smaller kitchen unit within the hotel. We also arranged hygiene training for the kitchen employees in particular, and the rest of the staff in general. The most difficult task we had was to persuade some of those kitchen staff that it was decidedly unhygienic for them to pee in the Open drains! The kitchens were closed in part for most of that summer and, gradually, the problem came under control. Unfortunately, despite all of our efforts, when the kitchens once again became fully operational the following year the epidemic of stomach illnesses reappeared.

The Thomson Organisation, which had become fearful that we were in danger of over-exposing the company, finally stopped our policy of hotel ownership in its tracks. By then, one way or another we had acquired seventeen hotels, with almost twelve thousand beds under our control and employing some two and a half thousand staff spread across a wide range of the Mediterranean resorts. I believe that, largely because of our incursion into the hotel sector, Thomson's was able to set the benchmark throughout the package tour industry for quality control. Our In hotel training programmes were of the highest professional standards, and eventually became the model that helped to improve standards across the board.

The seventies was the period when Thomson's started to feel more and more the intensity of the fierce competition from a company called Clarkson. Clarkson, as I have already mentioned, was a subsidiary of a public company that Managing Director, Tom Gullick, had expanded from a relatively small operator running trips to the Dutch bulb fields into a major competitor in the package tour industry. Their growth had come about because of what I described at the time as suicidal price discounting. Again I was reminded of the old truism in travel that 'anyone can give holidays away it, takes a little skill to be able to sell them'. And that is what Gullick was doing, effectively selling holidays with little or no margin. He had also entered into a long term and onerous contractual partnership with an airline called Court Line. Apparently, as it only became clear after the company's collapse, Clarkson was not merely guaranteeing Court Line a minimum number of flying hours on each of their giant Tri-

Star aircraft, thus enabling the airline to finance the acquisition of new generation planes, they were also guaranteeing that every Clarkson client would spend a minimum amount on duty free purchases on board. As a result Clarkson benefited from relatively cheap charter prices and thus grew at an alarming rate, forcing us at Thomson's to re-evaluate our pricing policy. Of course one of the inevitable problems that Clarkson was facing as a consequence of rapid growth was a totally inadequate infrastructure. They had no management organisation to speak of, the administration systems were reminiscent of our own a few years earlier and organisation in resort was either chaotic or non-existent. In turn that triggered off an unprecedented level of client dissatisfaction and Clarkson's was constantly in the headlines for all the wrong reasons.

At the time there was a live weekly television programme hosted by Bernard Braden and his wife, essentially dealing with consumer complaints rather like 'Watchdog' today. For weeks, every time the programme appeared, Bernard Braden would point towards an empty chair left vacant awaiting the arrival of Tom Gullick to answer the huge volume of client complaints. He never showed. We counter attacked Clarkson with our own vicious price cutting policy, using the strength of the Thomson Organisation to underpin us. It was a calculated, carefully worked out plan, structured with meticulous detail and incredibly risky. It turned out to be the beginning of the end for Clarkson. First they went under a couple of years later, thus forcing Court Line to absorb them to save their own operation and finally, not too long afterwards, Court line itself collapsed leaving thousands of passengers either stranded abroad or facing cancelled holidays.

It was a time of survival pricing for the larger companies and only the very fittest came through it. Horizon Holidays, another of the major players at the time albeit specialising in the more 'upmarket' sector, quickly followed Clarkson's into bankruptcy. That company had attempted to float itself on the London Stock Exchange but was refused permission, forcing it to float off its subsidiary, Horizon Midlands instead. It was the parent company that went into liquidation. Horizon Midland itself was eventually taken over, together with its charter airline, by Thomson. For the package tour industry as a whole it was a time of 'rationalisation', whatever that was supposed to mean. From Thomson's' point of view, it was simply a case of the survival of the fittest. Some of us survived, many did not. It was almost a weekly procession of bankruptcies and not a day went by without the industry being slated in the national press. But what I do remember, clearly, was that once again it was a time of chaos. The prices of package holidays rocketed as a result of the oil crisis and we were passing on price increases sometimes a matter of days prior to departure. Hundreds of thousands of clients were forced to cancel their holidays, often at short notice, by the unavoidable price hikes, and the industry was virtually brought to its knees by the uncertainty and the loss of revenue. Massive over bookings in the resorts were again heavily prominent as the Mediterranean hoteliers, panicked by the wholesale cancellations and the bad publicity, quickly turned to the German and Scandinavian markets to try to fill their beds. It became a battleground across the resorts as we fought to retain some semblance of quality (to say nothing of preserving our sanity!). If I complained earlier about the many sleepless nights I had to endure throughout the sixties, then that was like a hiatus compared to the trauma of 1973 and 1974. My staff and I ended the season in a state of total exhaustion. Nor could we understand the attack the press had waged on us that year through something that was completely outside of our control. To us it was interesting that not a single criticism was levelled against the oil companies when petrol prices absolutely rocketed. Perhaps we were a more exotic target?

The following year, wiser for the experience, and certainly the poorer, we considerably reduced our capacity but in the process had to make many of our staff redundant. Sales were sluggish as if the holiday public had become cautious, even mistrustful of the tour operators. As it was, the

summer of '74 started badly this time we were hit
with the French Air Traffic Control strikes, which
meant interminable delays at airports around
Europe. To make matters worse the strikes were
totally unpredictable which in turn required
passengers to sit literally for hours on end inside
suffocatingly hot aircraft while the captain waited
for a clearance 'slot' to over fly French airspace.
Week after week it went on with passengers
enduring insufferable conditions at airports and
on aircraft.

Finally the French authorities brought in the
military in an attempt to resolve the problem.
That proved to be a serious and fatal mistake; the
military controllers were simply too inexperienced
to handle the task and the exercise culminated in
a mid-air collision over France between two
Spanish aircraft: a scheduled Iberia flight en
route to London and a flight chartered by a
company called Spantax. The Spantax passengers
escaped unhurt but there were no survivors from
the Iberia flight. Three of my friends died in that
incident. Our Spanish Controller, Alberto Buena
Rivas, was actually booked to fly to London on the
Iberia flight but at the last minute had to cancel
due to pressure of work. That was his Guardian
Angel working for him. At last the strike ended,
possibly because of that mid-air collision, but it
was weeks before normal conditions prevailed.

Late that same summer I happened to be on
weekend duty at our London office when news

came through to us from Reuters that a DC 10 aircraft belonging to Turkish National Airlines had crashed shortly after take-off from Paris, bound for London's Heathrow Airport. Information about casualties was unclear and even contradictory. What we did know for certain was that Thomson had seventy-four passengers on board the flight and it was my duty, along with Norman Lewis, to fly immediately to Paris to visit the scene and hopefully help any survivors. Tragically, as I learned when I arrived at the crash site, there were unfortunately no survivors - some three hundred and fifty passengers on board were killed. After the tragedy I had witnessed some years ago at Stockport, which I described earlier, this disaster was without doubt the most distressing moment of my travel industry career. It was heart rending to look out on the fields of bodies and strewn personal belongings and luggage of the dead, scattered across the area like discarded rubble. And I shall always remember the eerie silence, which had descended over the site; to me it was as if the whole of the countryside had joined in the mourning.

It took a long time for me to adjust to that dreadful experience and to come to terms with the overwhelming sadness. I still shudder today when I think about it, and the last thing I am willing to do is to talk about it in detail. As a consequence of the disaster, the DCIO was grounded pending investigation; a number of previous incidents had suggested the possibility of a design fault. It transpired there was indeed a problem with one of the cargo doors, and, after a design refitting, the aircraft's airworthiness certificate was reinstated. I should point out that the DCIO albeit a much-advanced version has since flown hundreds of thousands of air miles and carried millions of passengers; in fact, it still remains one of my favourite aircraft.

1975 saw the death of General Franco and the re-introduction in Spain of a monarchy. The first unfortunate reaction we encountered was the resurrection of the trade unions who unleashed a wave of fierce and unrestrained militancy across Spain. We were badly affected, not only in our hotels, but also in the coach companies and the chain of travel agencies we owned throughout the country. Even the tour reps were involved, and regardless of the circumstances, it was impossible to discipline staff. Every hotel had its 'chapel' with a chain of command within the union. Daily, the management was issued with a set of outrageous demands, inevitably accompanied by the threat of strike action. One particular experience we had was with the Magalluf Park Hotel, one of our leased units. We wanted to close the hotel at the end of the season for refurbishing, but were informed that we couldn't do so without the permission of the relevant trade unions. We had no chance! However, one of the conditions of employment the unions had agreed with the

Government was not to strike without first giving the employer three full working days' notice. At that time, Roger Corkhill, whom I had appointed earlier that summer, managed the Thomson Hotels Division. Roger was having problems with the bars manager who he suspected of 'fiddling', so we decided to take a chance and sack him towards the end of the summer season. The rest of the staff staged an immediate 'walkout', thus unknowingly breaking their three- day strike agreement. Roger promptly sacked the lot of them, enabling us to close the hotel as planned. Then we had a strike amongst the Reps. It was one guy, who was employed at the Caribbean, who became a notorious left winger and who organised the Reps to strike – for what reason we never found out. Strangely enough the strike was lifted as the man was arrested.

Spain went into a period of intense mourning following General Franco's death. It came as a surprise to many that the old general had proved to be so popular given his reputation over the years for ruthlessness. Spain changed quite dramatically as a result: it quickly established a democratic political profile, something it had not experienced for almost forty years. Foreign investment increased substantially and a campaign of development and modernisation, of both business and infrastructure began in earnest.

The Package Tour Industry

The benefits for the package tour industry were immense; it wasn't merely that we saw a dramatic improvement in the road networks, but new hotels and other tourist attractions were springing up in all the major resorts expanding Spain's capacity for tourism virtually overnight. It was clear that the government was intent on establishing the country as a major player in tourism and the results were largely responsible for the unprecedented growth that occurred amongst package tour operators over the following years. Like the summer of 1961 before, that particular summer was labelled again, this time by another newspaper columnist as, another Summer of Discontent.' The reason for this was the unfortunate experience most of the bigger companies shared, of over optimism in the building of new hotels. Regrettably, many of them were not completed on time in fact some of them had not even been started! This resulted in thousands of Clients arriving in their resort either with no hotel accommodation or having to spend their holiday literally on a building site. It was a monumental disaster for the industry and the press, quite rightly, slated us. We somehow managed to struggle through that summer season and resolved never to let it happen again. It was noticeable that after that experience the legend 'artist's impression' disappeared completely from tour operators' brochures. It was another upward curve in our learning process.

CHAPTER TWENTY-SEVEN

COMING OF AGE

Throughout the seventies Thomson continued its policy of completely replacing the old propjet Britannias with the Boeing 737 fan jet aircraft. It was also in this period that the company made its first investment into the retail travel trade through the acquisition of the Lunn Poly Travel shops. A sophisticated 'real time' computer system had also been commissioned from IBM of America; when this finally came on stream in the late seventies it led the way for a dramatic change in the way the industry handled distribution. Effectively the new system enabled Thomson's to transform every travel agent into a direct line-booking agent, thus virtually obviating the need for telephone sales staff. It was a tremendous improvement in efficiency and cost savings, but one could not help but sympathise with the thousands of staff made redundant as a result. The rest of the industry quickly followed suit and administration efficiency soon became a watchword rather than a source of amusement.

In the late seventies Bryan Llewellyn gave notice that he was leaving the Travel Industry. What was not known at the time, and what was not made public, was he had more or less challenged Gordon Brunton to take over his job and become Chief Executive of the Organisation. He failed, miserably, and was transferred to run the book and magazine outfit. It was rather as he had done to me; he faced a humiliating future within the Thomson Organisation.

Prior to this I travelled with him to Jamaica, hosted by the then Minister of Tourism. The reason he came with me was to try to enlighten me with his own plans. I didn't take it on board. At the time we were in Negril and Llewellyn wanted to have supper at one of the local dining houses. Something bit me there, what it was I had no idea, but on the way back, going through New York, I started to develop a monumental thirst; I couldn't stop drinking water. We landed in Madrid where we were due to meet the Spanish Ministry of Tourism. I spent the night in a fever with the local hotel doctor trying to attend me but I was almost comatose. The next day we went to the meeting whereupon I passed out. When I came too I was on the way home; evidently I had a very high temperature caused by an unknown fever. In reality I should have gone to the Tropical Disease Hospital in London; I ended up in the local hospital in Hemel Hempstead.

When I came out of hospital I was then informed about Llewellyn leaving and I fully expected to get the job of Chief Executive. However, it transpired that as I did not have the pedigree to warrant such an appointment, the

Chief Executive job was given to John Sauvage, the Managing Director of Britannia Airways. He was a very nice man – I played golf with him on many an occasion – but he had very little idea of business practices. What Llewellyn wanted me to do was to take charge of all tour operations, other than Marketing, and I was to surrender the job of joint Managing Director. I refused, point blank. He couldn't understand my refusal; he was so used to getting his own way. Frantically, he searched around for some other job for me; he even offered me the job of running Lunn Poly in the Midlands; I doubt Nick Redfern would have appreciated that. In the end, and in despair, he left things as they were. I continued, as then the sole Managing Director of the company and Llewellyn left us to run his book-store in the Thomson Building!

It was shortly after that that he got the push from Thomson. What was it he used to say: "All management is transitory". He was certainly right in that respect as he bid us goodbye.

For me it was the beginning of the end; there was no way I could work with John Sauvage.

I left the Thomson Organisation at the end of the seventies to take over the then tiny operation of Club 18-30 where I remained for a number of years, successfully expanding the company and establishing its name in the marketplace before finally selling it on to Harry Goodman of ILG, the Intersun and Air Europe Leisure group. It was an interesting period in my travel career and one perhaps that may be worth the telling in the future, given the reputation and notoriety I helped to establish for Club 18-30.

But at that time we were witnessing the emergence of a package tour industry that bore little resemblance to its forerunners of the fifties and sixties when I had started. What had now evolved was a leaner and fitter industry, much more sophisticated and professional and the principal beneficiaries were the clients. Standards had changed beyond recognition by then; resort hotels had gone through a similar shakeout and many of those smaller units where we had experienced the problems of overbooking had all but disappeared. Charter aircraft companies were now fully modernised with fleets of fanjets. And at home the next generation of 'real time' computers were beginning to come on line. Graduate courses were introduced in the universities, allowing for the type of specialisation in the industry that we had never imagined could be possible. Appropriate training courses also became standard within the larger companies, bringing about even greater specialisation.

The government encouraging tour operators to considerably 'tone down' the exaggerated claims in their holiday brochures by introducing The Trade Description Act, although, frankly, it would be idealistic to assume the embellishments will ever entirely disappear,. As Norman Corkhill once said to me, all those years ago, 'It is within the very nature of our industry to oversell the product.'

So the package tour industry had truly come of age, and I was grateful for having had the opportunity to play a somewhat significant role in its development. No doubt in these modern times I will be regarded as something of a dinosaur myself with some of the young newcomers to the Industry; perhaps one day I might be classified as a 'Protected Species.' In the event they may be tempted to categorise me in that somewhat derisory category, I would ask them to reflect that without the Norman Corkhills and the Captain Langton's, and even the Vincent Cobbs, there would never have been an Industry to employ them.

The package tour industry itself will probably never expire; at least not in the way we understand it today. But even as I write the Industry is changing having been exposed by the Internet Services now available. Many people already have Villas or Apartments in the Med Resorts; now it is possible for them to reserve cheap discounted seats with the Budget Airlines, such as Easy Jet and Ryan Air – probably cheaper than the Package Tour Operators can offer. Also, clients are becoming more sophisticated; now they are able, should they so prefer, to reserve pretty well everything they require on the Internet that constitutes the ingredients for their holiday, and even today, the big Tour Operators are being discounted by the available opposition. But I do believe that would be Internet supporters should be mindful that in booking with Budget Airlines and making hotel reservations direct they will no longer have the benefit of ABTA Bonding if an airline goes bust – and this has happened in the past. In the last twelve months, as I write, this some three major airlines have gone to the wall. Fortuitously, there were no stranded passengers albeit two of the Airlines were not covered by the ABTA Bond, but they were 'Rescued' by other airlines who were, and still are, trying to avoid the reputation of being financially unsound.

OTHER BOOKS BY VINCENT COBB

An Angel's Kiss
Revelation
Contrition
Nemesis
No Hiding place

ABOUT THE AUTHOR

Vincent Cobb spent most of his working life in the Travel Industry, starting as a lowly paid clerk and part-time courier to the legendary Blackpool Landladies, graduating after many adventures to Joint- Managing Director of the giant Thomson Holidays.

It was his involvement in the television series, featured on ITV in January 2001, called Sun, Sex and Sangria, that prompted him to write the first of his novels, The Package Tour Industry, an anecdotal account that tells his story (by turns both hilarious and tragic) of the beginning of the Inclusive holiday business. But the darker side of Vincent has gone on to write firstly 'No Hiding place', a dark partly factual account of his early life in Blackpool, that tells the cathartic story of a violent father, an indifferent mother, and betrayal at the hands of the catholic church. .... now let his imagination chill you to the bone .

Vincent Cobb – Welcome to my World.

www.vincent-cobb.com

4061143R00160

Printed in Great Britain
by Amazon.co.uk, Ltd.,
Marston Gate.